THE SAGINAW HILLS

A drifter named Walter Bronson came upon
a beautiful girl bathing in a blue-water pond
on Senorio ranch, and without the faintest
idea he would become a fugitive from the
law with her as his accomplice, rode
innocently to the main ranch to get a riding
job. Sheriff Bob Nolan arrived at the ranch,
too, looking for a murderer whose
description fitted the newcomer called
Bronson, and that was when the trouble
started. It did not end until Bronson shot
and killed a renegade in the back-country of
the Saginaw Hills, and by then he and the
beautiful woman were more than just
friends.

THE SAGINAW HILLS

Frank Kimball

A Lythway Book

CHIVERS PRESS
BATH

First published in Great Britain 1981
by
Robert Hale Limited
This Large Print edition published by
Chivers Press
by arrangement with
Robert Hale Limited
1986

ISBN 0 7451 0322 7

British Library Cataloguing in Publication Data

Kimball, Frank
    The Saginaw Hills.—Large print ed.—
    (A Lythway book)
    I. Title
    823'.914[F]   PR6061.I4/

    ISBN 0–7451–0322–7

THE SAGINAW HILLS

CHAPTER ONE

Somewhere east of the tall-grass plateau, back through a heat-haze of stair-stepped mountains, probably at the base of that ice-sheen lying perpetually atop Mount Costillo, a rising spring fed that uneven watercourse which, when it finally left the mountains and crossed out over the grazing land, was known as Archer Creek, taking its name from Henry Archer who had first come onto the plateau more than fifty years earlier at the head of a longhorn cattle drive.

Henry had been dead now for thirty years, but the heritage he had left behind was rich in thousands of acres over which grazed hundreds of up-bred cattle tended by seasoned rangemen, under the old *segundo* Frank Ballinger. It was a large ranch, over one hundred and fifty thousand acres. It had been called the Senorio ranch for a half century, and although old Henry, Texas-born and reared, sniffed a little at a Mex title for his cow outfit, he had never used any other name because it pleased him, although he had never said so, to have his ranch named as though it were dukedom.

Archer Creek came close to the broad yard and in Henry's day had been the sole source of household and barnyard water. Since those times wells had been sunk so now the creek passed along, its functional purpose reverting to what it had been before, since time out of mind, a place where animals drank and where, occasionally, in the hot highland summers, men bathed after nightfall.

There was a magnificent pool eastward, across four miles of range where piney woods sheltered a wide cover. The pond was back in against some rising foothills about a mile. It was shaded by huge old pines whose summertime fragrance made the heat back up in there pleasantly bearable. For lack of a more appropriate name that cover and its pond were known as the Piney Woods, and since childhood it had been one of the favourite places of old Henry's children, and of their children, Beth and Barton Archer.

When Barton left Senorio for college, homesickness had shown through his cheerful letters home, especially when he lapsed into recollections of the Piney Woods.

Beth, two years younger than her brother, had never had to leave Senorio after graduating from secondary school. Her father, like old Henry before him, had a fixed idea about the place for women in this world. It had little to do with education, so Beth rode alone to the Piney Woods during hot lazy summer days. Earlier, her mother had accompanied her, then the housekeeper, a heavy-set dark Indian woman whose face and spirit were enduringly childlike

2

but whose body had grown increasingly round and massive as the years had accumulated.

Finally, after the death of her mother, followed four years later by the passing of her father, Beth and the Indian housekeeper went up there together, usually in a rig because the housekeeper, whose name was Jenny Plume, was by this time too large to sit a horse, let alone mount one, and finally Jenny remained at the main-house with her chores leaving Beth to go up there, less frequently now, by herself.

There were many memories at the pond; there were many memories in other places too, but in summertime the Piney Woods were special to Beth Archer.

She rode up there shortly before Barton returned from San Francisco, where he'd gone on Senorio business. It was a sultry, hot day with masses of cloud-galleons passing from northeast to southwest across a turquoise New Mexican sky.

Grizzled Frank Ballinger had watched her lope out of the yard, had waited briefly with his private thoughts, then had walked to the great log barn to pass the orders for the day.

Senorio kept ten steady riders, divided equally between native Mexicans, and men whose hides were nearly the same bronze colour from exposure, but whose eyes were more often than not, blue or grey. Frank was as at home speaking Spanish as English. No one knew how

3

old Frank Ballinger was, but Grandfather Archer had hired him. Nor did anyone, including Beth's father William, know Senorio as well as Frank did. He was both ageless and range-country-wise. He was a thin, angular, rawboned man of resolution and rawhide. In his day, those who were old enough to know said, Frank Ballinger had been a coldly deadly man to cross. But in Frank's youth, as in old Henry's time, there had been abundant reason for rangemen to be like that.

The Indian raiders were now gone. Occasionally *pillerias* still raced up out of Mexico to raid in the night, and there were always outlaws and fugitives, but there was less violence now than there had been, and if what remained did not seem less by some standards, most notably among easterners visiting New Mexico Territory, to oldtimers such as Frank Ballinger the country was adequately tamed, sound social order existed, and life was almost predictable.

At least when Frank parcelled out the work on this sultry day with the high clouds passing overhead, he had every reason to expect things would be accomplished according to his wishes, without incident, and as for Beth, she would go to the pond, swim up there in safety, and when she was hungry she would return. That was how life had been for years now, and there was no reason not to expect it to continue to be that way.

But—if trouble arrived, Frank Ballinger would handle it. He had achieved the age when nothing which could happen, had not happened before. As he had once said to Barton when they had roped a bogged mare out of a sump, any active man in range country who reaches fifty or sixty, has done whatever he is doing now, at least once before and in all probability he has done it many times before.

Some of the rangeriders were men nearly as old as Frank. Among those who lacked ten or twenty years of being his age, the squint, the leathery, weathered-dark skin, the deep lines and the knowledgeable eyes made them appear as old. They were all spare men whose lives no more turned upon the passage of years than their daily existence turned upon minutes or hours. They were suspended in a limbo of insularity. They arose early, worked the full day, returned in the evening, tired, yet looking forward to the days to come; time was important only as it became seasons of each year, otherwise it was neither significant to the men, nor very important.

Today, they had already assessed those huge clouds. It was not yet quite full summertime so there remained a possibility of showers. They altered their routine only to the extent of lashing slickers behind their cantles. Otherwise they rode forth in small groups as they always did,

5

and northeastward where Beth was riding, the sultry heat bore down more pressingly the closer she got to the pine-cove at the upper end of which lay the blue-water pond.

It always seemed hotter near the foothills. Today's heat was probably less than it had been a few days earlier, but it seemed more pressing because of its heavy humidity. By the time she was working back and forth among the sidehill pines toward the pond, keeping out of direct sunlight by taking this circuitous route up there, she was perspiring and red in the face, for although her colouring was golden rather than white—old Henry's second wife by which he'd had his only offspring had been a half-Delaware woman—and she tanned rather than sunburned, she was not impervious to this particular variety of heat.

Then the pond appeared through the trees, with its backdrop of pine-slopes and its nearer broad fringe of dark grass and myriad small wildflowers, and she slackened gait to appreciate as she always had, this magnificent, secluded place with its unchanged beauty and its soft, gentle hush broken only infrequently by bird-calls from farther back.

Where she came down to the dazzling sunsmash and out of the trees the grass was hock-high and forming seed-heads which seemed to over-burden the lean stalks so that any vague breeze made the grass ripple, sometimes bluish-green, sometimes emerald-green.

She off-saddled, hobbled the horse, tossed down the blanket and bridle, and went over to the solitary round boulder upon the west side of the pond, and stood gazing at the reflections of clouds out across the water. It was too hot now, too late in the day, for trout to be feeding, so the water lay undisturbed over its ten-acre surface, and probably if Beth Archer had been more observant she would have also noticed the stillness. Not a bird was back yonder up the foothill slope along the uneven northward country.

She dropped her hat in the grass, kicked out of her boots and sat on the white-veined boulder trailing her feet in the water.

This place had a uniquely therapeutic effect, it always had. She'd come here as a child with her worries, her depths of sorrow—as when her mother had died—and she had come here later when she'd been troubled by a peculiar restlessness. It had always soothed, and many times it had healed, and never once had it failed to restore her.

Today, with the muggy heat and the stillness, she watched her reflection, felt the cool water, and looked around once or twice to find her horse. The animal was perfectly content in the half-shade back yonder, cropping grass and indifferently switching its tail.

A cloud obscured the sun, the land became duskily shadowed, and Beth waded out into the water, paused to tie her yellow neckerchief around her hair, then dived under, came up five yards from the boulder, swam with powerful strokes mid-way, dived and turned, surfaced and swam back.

When she stood up in the shallows, riding britches and blouse plastered to the strong roundness of her body, the sun returned—and a man was leaning in the shade beside a fragrant pine tree, watching.

When their eyes met it was like an electric shock. Beth Archer had never had this happen before, at the pond. She was simultaneously surprised, acutely self-conscious, and angrily embarrassed.

He said, 'You beat me to it. I was going to do the same thing,' then he sauntered down beside the rock and smiled at her.

There was no place to run to, no place to hide; the embarrassment was holding her in one place as though she were a stone statue.

He was a man of average height with smoky blue eyes, a round chin and a straight mouth which was now lying softly curved in a smile. He was handsome in a way which seemed both strong and sensitive, both masculine and tolerant.

There was nothing she could do now, so she loosened the yellow neckerchief, shook her hair free and without looking at him walked up out of the water to the boulder, and sat down. Then she said, 'You have no business here.'

He sank down in the grass looking up at her. 'I guess not,' he agreed mildly. 'My name's Walter Bronson.' He threw a glance towards the eastward slopes. 'I left the stageroad yesterday and rode west—reached this place last night and made a camp up yonder in the trees.' His smoke-blue gaze drifted back to her, the smile returning, wider this time. 'A saddle-tramp.'

She continued to look out across the pond, profiled to him, golden, clothes moulded to her, full-bodied and lovely. 'I'm waiting for you to leave,' she said quietly.

He also turned to gaze out over the pond. For a while he was silent, then he leaned to arise as he said, 'I'm sorry. I didn't do it on purpose. I didn't know anyone was out here until I saw the horse, then saw you swimming back.'

She drew up both knees and encircled them with her arms, dropped her head a little and continued to sit there looking dead ahead as though he did not exist.

He stood up, hesitated briefly studying her, then turned back toward the westward trees. She did not move until his sound was no longer audible. Then she wanted to turn and look, instead she sat perfectly motionless letting the sunlight begin the slow drying process.

She felt almost betrayed; as though the spirits

9

or fates or destinies which lived in this private place, had protected her privacy all through the years—up until today—then had become abruptly indifferent.

It was a sad sensation because she had always felt absolutely safe and shielded in this place, and now she would never be able to feel that way again.

She was dry enough in an hour and a half to tug back into her boots, go saddle up and head for the home place. By then, the orange sun had mellowed to its late-day tones and there were shadows coming forth around the pond from the horseshoe-shaped lift and fall of forested hills.

CHAPTER TWO

She told Frank Ballinger about Walter Bronson on Wednesday, and on Thursday her brother drove into the yard, using the same top-buggy he had used to depart in, and which during the interim had been parked in Webster Rudell's corralyard out behind the liverybarn in Marietta.

Barton looked fit. He usually did look that way. He was taller than his sister had the same black hair and dark eyes, the same faintly golden skin-tones and the same even, good features.

Frank shook Barton's hand and smiled, two sure signs that he was pleased. They went to the long veranda of the main-house, smoked, had some branch-water and whiskey, and talked until mid-afternoon. Then Frank went thoughtfully back down to the yard, and when Beth rode in from the south range—where the loose saddlehorses were kept this time of year—it was evening and Barton was back out there on the veranda, having been fed by Jenny Plume, freshly bathed and attired, and smoking a fragrant cigar. He watched her cross from the barn, sighed, and when she came up onto the porch and saw him in the shadows she made a little throaty sound of delight and went over to lean and kiss his prematurely greying temple.

He smiled and watched her settle against the railing in front of his chair. She was a beautiful woman. She had not been a beautiful sister when they had been growing up—or maybe she had been and he'd failed to notice it. Now, as he removed the cigar he said, 'Out in San Francisco women carry parasols so they won't get wrinkled skin from exposure.'

She eyed him askance. He had teased her ever since she could remember, which she tolerated well, but she had never during all those years been able to determine when he was, and when he was not, doing it.

'You can't tell whether I have wrinkles tonight,' she replied, then stared at him. 'Bart—

11

not a *parasol*!'

He laughed. 'Why not? Think how elegant you'd look riding to the Piney Woods pond, or after the horses with a parasol in your hand.'

'I'll brain you with it!'

He considered the cigar. 'In anticipation of some such barbaric reaction—no—I brought you a lace dress though and a cameo choker, and some other odds and ends ... Beth—I think we'd ought to sell that copper stock paw bought when we were kids. I had an offer for it in San Francisco. I told them I'd discuss it with you, and write them our answer.'

She was equal owner in Senorio, but she and Barton had an easy arrangement. As like as not they discussed important matters while cow-hunting or bringing in the loose-stock, or during a breather during the branding and altering, which had been completed last month.

She rarely argued with him. Her interest in Senorio was deeply inbred, but her brother was a college-trained administrator, which was perfectly agreeable to her. She was not by nature either domineering, or competitive with Barton.

Now, she simply said, 'Why? Do we need the money?'

He shook his head. 'No. I just don't have much faith in things I can't see or touch, or control. That stock rises, then drops, then plugs along, then drops or rises again. I'm not satisfied we should keep it when we've got a hell

12

of a strong offer.' He plugged the cigar back into his mouth. 'It's up to you.'

She knew less than he did about stock, and, like him, had matured with the feeling that things people could not see or control were untrustworthy. The weather for example, or the politics of the Territorial capital, or of the National capital.

'Sell it,' she said, and brushed that aside to then say, 'For the first time in my life, I met someone at the blue pond.'

'Who?'

'A . . . he called himself a saddle-tramp, but he didn't look like one. A stranger.' She considered her scuffed boot-toes. 'I was swimming and when I came back to the rock— he was standing there.'

Barton's dark gaze remained dead level. 'Swimming?'

She reddened, which he failed to see because of the dusk. 'Not like *that*. I had my britches and a blouse on. . .' She remembered exactly how she had looked, clothes plastered to her, and dropped her gaze to the boots again. 'But that's the first time. . . In all the years I've been going up there.'

He smoked a moment, then said, 'I suppose there've been drifters pass through up there from time to time, Beth. This time one of them came down where you saw him. Did you tell Frank?'

'Yes. But I don't know whether he sent anyone up there or not.'

Barton's interest lapsed. 'Frank said we don't have the calf-crop we should have this year.'

Beth knew the answer to that. 'Those pedigreed bulls we brought in last year were raised on soft grass, Bart.'

He looked at her. 'Sore-footed?'

'I told you last summer that most of the time when I rode out, they'd be standing in the mud along the creek. I'd drive them out to the cows, and they'd go back to the mudholes. I wanted to tell Frank to have them brought in and shod.'

'Why didn't you, Beth?'

She gazed steadily at her brother. 'You know why. I doubt if a woman ever told Frank Ballinger anything. Not even his mother.'

'You're an owner,' Barton said. 'Woman or not.'

She straightened up off the porch railing. 'Next time *you* tell him.' She smiled as her brother removed his cigar, which had died. 'Men are always right and women are—just women. Paw was like that. Grandfather also was... You're a little like that, Bart, but Frank...' She shook her head, still smiling.

For Barton this topic, like the saddle-tramp at the Piney Woods pond, was irrelevant to his primary—his only real—interest, which was the efficient function of Senorio ranch. 'I'll ride out with Frank tomorrow,' he said, the implication

14

being that he would discuss the matter of the sore-footed bulls but not the fact that Beth had known the pedigreed bulls were not staying with the cows.

She twisted to look down the broad, quiet yard. Lights showed from the bunkhouse windows and there was a wood-fire in the stove; the fragrance of wood-smoke came up as far as the main-house.

Jenny Plume had once told her she was not forceful enough; that men were like oaks, strong and thick; that if Jenny had learned nothing else in fifty years it was that women were like mares, quicker to perceive, to learn, and to know how to remedy things.

Beth smiled in the night thinking back to that moment when she and Jenny had sat in the warm kitchen talking. Then Beth faced her brother again, still with a hint of a smile down around her heavy, soft mouth. She had never wanted to be forceful. It was not her nature to be that way. As she regarded Barton he said, 'Anything else I should know?'

'The range studs are old, Bart. They're breeding back. In a few years we'll have the runtiest, least intelligent horses in the country.'

He hoisted both feet to a bench and crossed both hands over his stomach gazing at her. 'All right. I'll look around over the next month or so. What else?'

'We need a horse-breaker.'

15

'What's the matter with Manuelito? He's broken Senorio horses since we were kids and no one turns out a better saddle animal.'

'How long has it been since we were kids, Bart?'

He sat for a moment without speaking, then sighed and pulled his feet down off the bench to sit straighter. 'Yes, I suppose that's right.' He smiled in the darkness. 'You think I should ride out more.'

'You should.'

He stood up. He was a good-looking man with the same even, strong features she had, except that in Barton they were more composed in strength, in masculine confidence. 'But running Senorio takes more time at a desk than in a saddle, you know.'

She smiled at him. 'I know. I'm not blaming you for anything.' They entered the big old house and stood briefly in the lighted parlour where two oil portraits, one of their father, the other of old Henry, hung above the great stone fireplace.

He said, 'I missed this place. For a city, San Francisco is fine, but it's noisy and has too many people.' He showed her a rueful grin and went off into his end of the house leaving her standing in the parlour where shadows lurked in far corners.

His talk of San Francisco no more interested her than her talk of the saddle-tramp at the pond

16

had interested him.

They could meet easily and understandingly in the middle ground, which was Senorio, the vast feudal holding which had always been their personal world.

Beth returned to the veranda in the warm summer night to lean upon an upright-post and watch eerie clouds pass. The bunkhouse was dark, there was not a sound anywhere throughout the big yard, or beyond it. There was no movement either. It was a little like being the only living thing in the world, to stand alone out there tonight.

The riders had brought in fresh horses. They had also turned out the studs, the idea being, as it had always been on Senorio, that the loose-stock broodmares would produce their next colt crop just short of a year hence, when the weather would be warm with plenty of grass for the mares to convert to rich horse-milk.

Beth knew every one of those stallions by name and there were close to twenty of them. She had once sweetly asked Frank how old the youngest stud was, and he had muttered something indistinguishable because Frank Ballinger was of that generation which could not bring itself to discuss studs and their purpose with womenfolk.

She had mouthed some of those stallions. Every one of them was smooth-mouthed. Not only that, but the bloodlines were inextricably

17

confused by now.

Her father had once told her he would have been satisfied with what the Fates had given him if they had only made her a boy.

Well, they hadn't, she told herself while leaning out there tonight, and that was that. Also, while she'd wished many times during her gangling years that they *had* made her a boy, over the last four or five years she had been less inclined to think that way, but why she felt differently now, she could not have explained even to herself.

A couple of horses squealed crankily in the corrals out behind the barn, then were silent. Beth's final glance was off in the direction of the Piney Woods. If it remained muggy she would ride back up to the pond—but this time she would also scout up the countryside before going down for a swim.

CHAPTER THREE

By nature as well as early training, Beth was an early-riser, an uncommon attribute in women. Jenny Plume had once said the only early-risers in this world were people with bad consciences, and Beth had laughed so hard Jenny had finally smiled.

This morning Jenny was making delightful

18

aromas come out of the kitchen by the time Beth was dressed, which was a little odd, so when Beth went out there Jenny, who knew both the Archers better than they knew themselves, turned and gestured with a large wooden ladle. 'Your brother'll need Senorio food after being down in that big city. A man can't work on frog legs and poached eggs.'

Beth was one of those individuals who could eat like a horse and never gain an extra pound. Jenny was just the opposite; she had once said that she gained weight, some mysterious way, just by inhaling the fragrance of food. Her face was perfectly round, without a line in it although she was well into her fifties, and her sloe-eyes were bright, knowing and wise.

She had dimples, which may have been the reason she looked to be no more than perhaps eighteen or twenty, and she had a delightful sense of humour, along with a degree of perception which had over the years imbued her with a philosophical outlook.

As she fed Beth she said, 'Some of the men are going over to the Marietta range today,' and when Beth looked enquiringly upwards, Jenny also said, 'There aren't any cattle over there.'

Beth faintly frowned. 'Then why—?'

'Because they are men, that's why. They'll lope into town.'

'Frank doesn't know it,' Beth said quickly and Jenny gazed at the younger woman. 'He's

19

going along. Manuelito needs some more medicine.' Jenny returned to the wood-stove. 'Even the old bucks sneak away now and then.'

'My brother wants to ride out with Frank this morning,' Beth said, going to the stove to re-fill her coffee cup.

'Then he'd better get out there, because I heard them talking last night. They're going to ride out early.'

They did; by the time Barton reached the yard Frank had assigned the daily work and only one rider was still in the yard. He had to remain behind to shoe some horses.

Beth's horse was also gone. Barton asked the rider if he had seen her leave and the man spat amber, pointed northwesterly, and said, 'Half hour ago, Mister Archer,' then went back to his forge.

Barton went over to the barn, rigged out a using horse from the back corrals and also rode northwesterly. There was not much point in heading for the Marietta range; it was huge and a person could ride all day over there and not find anyone.

The morning had a faint hint of an earlier chill to it, but at least those immense clouds were gone, the sky was pale blue and flawless, so as the morning advanced there would be heat.

Barton's mood was not the best. He resented the fact that Frank had not waited for him, even though when they had parted yesterday Barton had made no mention of wanting to ride with Frank today.

His sister's mood was different. She rarely got angry and this morning with a fresh, strong horse beneath the saddle, a clear sky and something in mind, she loped across the dawn-lighted range as a free spirit. She had never been denied this freedom, even as a child.

The Senorio loose-stock ordinarily grazed across several thousand acres closer to the far hills than the cattle went. Later, when the native grasses went to seed and turned dry, the horses would drift southward, but this was late spring, early summer, there was an abundance of feed in all directions.

She saw no horses until the sun was climbing and she had covered six or seven miles, then it was a little band of mares with gangling colts, and at sight of her the mares herded their foals ahead and fled. Ordinarily they would simply have thrown up their heads and watched, but now their maternal instinct made them act differently.

Beth made little attempt to catch them. She loped parallel, several hundred yards to one side of the band, and when they saw her make no move to head them off or to swerve closer, the mares with the newest foals slackened off. Eventually all the mares slowed, then halted.

Beth rode another dozen yards then also halted. She swung facing the wary mares, fished in her saddle-pockets, brought forth a pair of small binoculars and made a leisurely study.

All but two mares had colts by their sides; those two were large and springy. Beth studied the colts and from long experience could name the father of each foal. She was satisfied, shoved the binoculars back into the saddle-pocket, lifted her reins and continued northward, closer to the foothills to look for other loose-stock.

She found two separate bands, one with all the colts on the ground, the second band with half the mares yet to foal. The second band fled, awkwardly and not very swiftly because those heavy mares were unable to make much speed, but she loped parallel as she had done before looking over there—and had no idea she was in the midst of a prairie-dog town until her horse sank a hind foot to the pastern through a thin topping of earth. She was raising her left hand to bring him down to a walk when he fell though the next roofing over a prairie-dog tunnel, and this time he could not extricate his hoof in time.

He went down in a grunting roll, end over end. Beth kicked free by instinct. When the horse tipped far over she sailed ahead and to one side. Even so the up-ended horse came down beside her, atop the saddle, then rolled to his right. She was on his left, stunned but instinctively trying to force her dazed body to respond. It did not do more than allow her to partially rise, then fall back.

22

The sensation was like rushing down a long dark tunnel in full blackness. At the end of the tunnel there was an abrupt halt—then nothing.

The horse got back to his feet, and miracle of miracles he had not broken his ankle, he had not even sprained it. But he was frightened and stood there shaking, looking left and right as though seeking whatever had caused the fall, shaking from one end to the other. When he saw the horseman coming he watched intently. Perhaps another time he would have raised his head and fled, but he was still numb with astonishment, so he stood watching, while very gradually the shock began to pass, the quaking lessened, and by the time the rider got close, hauled down to a halt and swung off, the disoriented animal was beginning to recover.

The rider left his mount beyond the tell-tale piles of dirt, went across to Beth and sank to one knee to roll her over and make a swift examination. The first she knew she was not alone, or even where she was or what had happened, was when someone with thick shoulders leaned enough to protect her eyes from sunlight, and she looked up.

He smiled, wagged his head and said, 'From a mile out it looked like you'd landed on your head. I thought you'd be dead.'

She knew the face, the thick upper body, and the smile. She said, 'You're trespassing.'

He shoved back his hat, fished a small bottle

from a pocket, hoisted her into half a sitting position, pulled the cork with his teeth and poured whiskey down her. She choked, water sprang to her eyes and for a moment she could not draw a breath. Then she coughed and could not stop coughing. He balanced her against his leg, re-corked the bottle and shoved it back into a pocket. Then he placed a hand between her breasts over her heart, pushed steadily inward with considerable force, and suddenly pulled back the hand. She stopped coughing.

Panting, with dust on her cheeks and dirt in her hair, with watering eyes and feeling as breathless as though she had been running hard, she could do nothing but blink upwards at him.

This *wasn't* the Piney Woods pond. She was not still up there with him. This was... She weakly turned to look around, saw her horse with the askew saddle, with dirt and grass-stain over them both, and as she gradually remembered, she saw the distant band of mares.

Bronson ... Walter Bronson. She waited until her breathing was almost normal then said, 'I tried to haul back—but it was too late. My horse...?'

'All right. But most folks look ahead where they're riding.'

She couldn't argue with that, but she *could* explain. 'I was looking at those mares. When I realised we were in the middle of a 'dog town, it was too late.'

24

'Are you all right? Can you move your feet and legs and arms?'

She tried it, very carefully. Her body was sore, she was dishevelled with several buttons torn off her shirt. She raised a hand to push back some black hair and leaned against his leg. 'I'm all right, Mister Bronson,' she said.

He grinned. 'You don't drink much whiskey, do you?'

She smiled a little. 'No. And I'm not sure I needed it.'

He steadied her, then pulled away to arise and go look at her horse. In his absence she found the torn buttonholes, and swiftly made some arrangements to hold the blouse closed. Had he noticed? Probably. He was a man, wasn't he? She turned to watch him handle her horse, his back to her, and thought each time they met she was—well—not presentable.

He strolled back and stood smiling at her. 'You're lucky. When you get home you could turn that horse out for a few days. He's not hurt but he's bound to have some strains.' He sank down beside her. 'Another shot of whiskey?'

At the look she gave him he laughed. 'None of it tastes good, I guess, but under some circumstances it doubles for medicine. Do you want to stand up?'

She wasn't quite ready. 'No. In a few minutes.' She regarded him. 'I thought you'd ridden on through?'

'No. I changed camps though, so it wouldn't bother your swimming.' He pointed. 'I've got a place up yonder through the trees a ways.' He dropped the arm. 'This morning I rode down here when I saw the horses. Just to look. I'm not a horsethief.'

His eyes twinkled. Without knowing anything about him she knew he was good-natured and even-tempered. The whiskey was working. She had swallowed twice, in self defence, otherwise she would have gagged or drowned. At least she had felt as though those things would happen when he'd been solicitously pouring the gawd-awful stuff down her throat.

She owed him something so she said, 'I'm glad you came along, Mister Bronson.'

'Maybe this will make up for intruding the other time,' he replied, shifting his gunbelt and holstered Colt so he could ease down lower in the grass beside her. 'What's your name?'

She hesitated, but only shortly, then said, 'Beth Archer.'

He accepted that with a little nod. 'My sister's name. Beth. She died four years ago.'

'I'm sorry, Mister Bronson.'

'So was I. She was all the family I had left.'

'Was it an accident?'

'No. Childbirth. She married a blacksmith back in Kansas. This would have been their first child.'

26

'The baby died too?'

'Yes.' His head came up and while the kindly look was in his gaze, behind it there was something else, something more haunting.

Beth changed the subject. 'We're a little behind with some of the foaling mares this year. That's what I was doing out here this morning. Looking at them.'

His blue-grey eyes drifted beyond, out where the horses were beginning to graze away. 'I looked at them earlier, about sunup. The heavy ones aren't more than a week or two off.' He dropped his eyes to her face. 'You're part of this ranch?'

'Yes. It's called Senorio. My grandfather founded it.'

He kept gazing at her. 'You're an owner, then?'

'Half. With my brother Bart.'

He swung to look out where his horse was, then over at her horse, and finally as he leaned to arise he turned back toward her. 'I'll ride on this afternoon. You won't have to send anyone to run me off.' He stood up and held out a hand to her. As she accepted and came up, slowly, clinging to his hand, she said, 'We don't do that... Run people off... When I first saw who you were, I thought I was back at the pond. That's where I remembered you from.'

He held her hand and waited to be sure she was steady on her feet. 'I'll ride on anyway. I've

27

never seen the Wickenburg country. Figured I might go over there this season.'

She did not free her fingers. 'By the time you get over there the riding season will be finished.'

'This is my loafing summer, Miss Archer.' His smile returned, gently. 'I work three and loaf one ... I know; a man can't get ahead doing that. But he sure sees a lot of beautiful country and ...'

She freed her hand and avoided his gaze. 'It's your life, Mister Bronson.' She looked back and smiled at him. 'In a way I envy you. Being a man ... things are different for men.'

He gestured. 'This is all yours. You couldn't duplicate it this side of heaven. I've seen a lot of country so you can take my word for it.' He raised a hand, plucked a limp grass-stalk from her hair and dropped it. 'If you'd like I could ride part way back to make sure you're able to make it.'

She had a forthright answer on her lips. She was perfectly able; she needed no help. She said, 'I'd appreciate that,' and as he nodded and turned to go after the horses she stared after him with her mouth open. That had not been at all what she had meant to say.

CHAPTER FOUR

She saw Barton coming from a great distance. She hadn't grown up with him to be unable to tell him that far off from the way he sat a saddle. She turned abruptly eastward and without comment Walter Bronson followed along. Why, exactly, she did not want to meet Barton right now was something else she could not have sensibly explained to herself.

They loped along parallel to the backgrounding hills, and evidently Barton did not notice them. He was probably doing what she had been doing earlier, looking for brood-mares. Or possibly that dark background camouflaged them. In either case Beth kept to a long lope until they were within cannon-shot distance of the Piney Woods, then she led the way with thorough familiarity up through the broken country, in and out among the giant pine trees, and down the far slope where the horseshoe-shaped clearing was, and her companion recognised the pond before they rode out into open country.

He was puzzled. 'You live around here?'

She reddened. 'No.' She raised an arm. 'The home-ranch is down there.' She offered no additional explanation and kept ahead so he would not see her red face. But when they broke clear and passed across the tall-grass meadow in the direction of the pond she said, 'I wanted to wash the dirt off.'

He did not say a word, but where she swung off he hobbled both the horses, loosened the cinchas and removed the bridles under her watching gaze. She took him over to the big old stone where they had first met.

He said, 'Go ahead. I'll sit with my back to the rock.'

She didn't dare. Not with those buttons gone from her blouse, but she was tempted anyway. Instead, she knelt beside the nearest little clear-water inlet, pushed up her sleeves and washed.

He watched her, admired the way her body moved and how it drew the cloth taut at thigh and breast. She was a beautiful woman, but one thing about her troubled him.

When she sat back with water dripping from her face, and smiled, he said. 'Feel better?'

She did indeed feel better. 'Yes.'

He saw her turn and glance across the clear, pale water. It was hot out where they were, the sun was directly above them. 'Go ahead and dive in,' he told her, and moved back into the meagre shade of the big boulder, eased down with a grunt and settled his back to the stone, then tipped down his hat, fully composed to grant her full and unobserved freedom.

She looked over her shoulder, and laughed because he looked so resigned, the way Jenny had looked when she had sat in that exact place when Beth had been a gangling child and had not been allowed to come up here to swim without Jenny being along.

He thumbed up his hatbrim and turned. 'I missed something?'

She arose, went over and sat down near him to explain about Jenny Plume and how his attitude had reminded her of those earlier days. He was a good listener. When she had finished he said, 'No parents?'

'No. They died years ago. Jenny is as big as a horse, and wonderful. She's a Delaware woman.' Looking steadily at him she then said, 'My grandmother was half Delaware.'

'I didn't know they were in New Mexico.'

'They weren't. They're a homeless people. The ones who came here arrived as army scouts and messengers. There are a few half-breeds still around. Over in Marietta and among the ranches.'

He said, 'Your grandfather . . . ?'

'A Texan. After the Civil War he left the South.'

Bronson nodded. 'Yeah. A lot of them did . . . Miss Archer—go ahead and cool off, I won't look.'

She arose to her knees. 'Come with me.'

He blinked. 'I—don't know how to swim.'

That had not occurred to her even though she knew most of the Senorio rangeriders had at one

31

time or another admitted that they could not swim either. She said, 'I'll teach you.'

He cocked an eye at the position of the sun to estimate the time of day, then raised a limp sleeve to push off sweat. 'I'll tell you the gospel truth, Miss Archer—I'm downright uneasy around a lot of water. Like that pond yonder.'

She grabbed his hand, sat back to stand up, and as she pulled she said, 'All right. You wade and I'll swim. Come along.'

He accompanied her to the far side of the big rock and while he had admired the lake earlier, because of its beautiful setting, now he eyed it differently.

She kicked out of her boots, used her bandana to hold her hair back, and emptied her pockets into one boot. He watched all this and finally said, 'I guess you don't have to do much laundry that way.'

She smiled. 'When I come out of the water . . . don't look.'

He was still nodding when she arched high off the boulder and shot ahead out beyond the narrow band of shallow water. He marvelled at her grace, but mostly he admired the power she'd exhibited to do that.

Then he dutifully sat down to remove his boots and roll up his trouser-legs. The water was cold. Colder than he had expected it to be, so while the sun beat down from above, his feet and ankles were chilled, and this, he told

32

himself, is what people do because they like it. Hell! The best way to utilise water when a man needed to bathe was to find a shallow creek where the water would be warm, and sit in it.

Beth surfaced, spat water, and watched his timorous progress. She wanted to laugh but instead she turned, up-ended and dived far down, rolled over and shot back toward him five feet down.

When she surfaced this time his lips were working through an expression of sharp pain. He had stepped upon a pointed little stone. She *did* laugh this time, and he turned, shaking his head.

She waited until he was several yards distant, wading along with his back to her, then slid out of the water, got upon the hot grass and lay face down. Her body was sore from the fall earlier, but she was a muscular, surprisingly durable individual. She rested her face upon an outflung arm and closed her eyes.

There was not a breath of air stirring. Heat worked through her clothes to gradually relax every part of her body. She loved these moments almost as much as she enjoyed the exercise of swimming.

By the time Walter Bronson abandoned his wading and came gingerly back across the grass to the vicinity of the big boulder, Beth was asleep. He looked at her, leaned to be sure, then sat down and rubbed his feet, which were as white and tender as were the feet of all rangemen. He never went barefoot, hadn't done anything like that since he'd been a child.

Then he rolled a smoke, lit it, leaned back with his exposed toes absorbing welcome sun-heat, and gazed across the pond. The sun had moved, but not very much. Their hobbled horses were full now and stood head-to-tail as though they had known each other for years, desultorily switching their tails to keep bot flies from entering each other's nostrils.

Bronson finished his smoke and considered his dry feet. They looked healthy; pink now and even the stone bruise was forgotten. A voice nearby said, 'If you don't put your boots on, Mister Bronson, you're going to wish you had.'

He looked over where she was lying with her head propped upon one arm, gazing at him. She said, 'Sunburn. Look at them.'

He reached for his socks and boots. She continued to watch him and he could feel it. When he was shod again he lay back, looked straight up at the faded sky and tipped his hat down over his eyes and he said, 'My name is Walter.'

She did not respond to that, so for a time they were both silent. Then he spoke again from beneath his hatbrim. 'You're a good swimmer.'

'I've been swimming up here since I was a child. My father taught me. We used to bring food with us . . . Mister Bronson?'

34

'Yes.'

'Are you hungry? I have two sandwiches in my saddlebags.' She did not wait for his response but sprang up and went out to her horse. He rolled over to watch her walk out, then walk back. She was the most magnificent woman he had ever seen. He rolled back to look straight up, and as she knelt and unwrapped a squashed sandwich he said, 'My name is Walter.'

She leaned to hand him a sandwich. He turned and their eyes met. The torn buttonholes were still torn. He kept his eyes upon her face and as he accepted the ruined squashed sandwich he said, 'My name is Walter.'

She laughed at his expression. 'The next time I'll make sure the horse falls on the other saddle-pocket.'

He continued to look at the sandwich so she sat back on her heels and said, 'Don't you like beef sandwiches?'

His head came up. 'I like them. That's not what I was wondering about.'

'The relish on it?'

'No. Why aren't you married?'

She sat utterly still for a long time, then she ducked her head and became busy removing the gingham napkin from her smashed sandwich.

He groped for a way out and finally said, 'Excuse me. It's just been in my mind is all. I shouldn't have said it.'

35

Her eyes came back to his face. She bit into the sandwich, looking steadily at him. 'Sometimes in winter there's a foot of snow around the pond.'

He took the rebuke well. 'I guess there'd be two or three feet back up along those mountainsides.' He chewed and swallowed. 'That's good beef.'

'We never kill them right off grass. We always grain them out for about three months. My father used to say you couldn't do that and sell them, or you'd lose money, but for his family it was different.'

Bronson ate, listened, said nothing, and when he'd finished he smiled at her. 'Thanks. I trapped three grouse at my camp yesterday, but they're not as good as beef.'

She settled her back against the big rock and looked out where the horses were dozing. 'I never think about it,' she said quietly. 'I *have* thought about it, of course. All women do. But . . .'

'Beef being better than grouse?'

She did not change position nor raise her voice. 'You know exactly what I mean.'

He watched the slow, full rise and fall of her upper body as she sat over there, almost completely dry now. He knew what she meant but he did not know what he was supposed to say, or if he was supposed to say anything at all. He also wished he'd kept his bafflement to

36

himself because now there was a distinct awkwardness between them. Before, it had been so easy and pleasant; they both had roughly the same disposition, and that had made it easy.

She turned slowly looking him squarely in the eye. 'Why aren't you?'

He fished for his bandana and elaborately wiped the same fingers he'd just finished wiping in the grass. 'Just never got around to it, I guess... Yes, I've thought about it too, now and then.' He tucked away the bandana. 'But with me it's a lot different.'

'How?'

'Well, to start with, a rangeman's wages won't support a family, and then there's the moving around.'

'Mister Bronson, we have riders on Senorio who have been here all their working lives. They don't move around.'

'Any married ones?'

'Yes. Some of the older men. The Mexicans. They have families in town.'

He met her gaze. 'Do you like to argue?'

She flushed, then shook her head. 'No. And I wasn't arguing with you.'

He crookedly smiled at her. 'Sure did sound like it ... Miss Archer, it's just no life for a woman, being married to a rangerider, and you know it as well as I do.' He continued to smile. 'And that ends the argument.' He lay back in the grass, placed his hat to shield his eyes again, and waited.

He heard her moving over against the rock and when she said nothing he lifted part of his hat and peeked. She was lying flat out again, on her stomach, with her face resting upon one arm. If they both slept, which would be very easy to do now, when they awakened it would be dusk. He still had to strike camp and she undoubtedly should be back at the home-ranch before nightfall.

He said, 'This has been the most interesting day of my life.'

Her eyes sprang open facing him across the small distance.

'And if I go to sleep out here I won't be able to ride on until tomorrow . . . And if we both sleep your brother'll be combing the range for us— and he'll shoot me.'

'My brother,' she retorted, 'has never shot anyone. He hasn't even shot *at* anyone. And if you don't strike your camp until tomorrow, what difference will it make? Wickenburg will still be over there.'

He crinkled his eyes at her. 'You *do* like to argue.'

She raised her head slightly and regarded him without speaking for a moment, then dropped it back down again as she said, 'I apologise.' She pushed her face into the grass so that her further words had a slightly muffled sound. 'Mister Bronson . . .?'

'Yes'm.'

'We'll hire you.'

'Miss Archer, this is my loafing summer, remember?'

She waited a moment then said, 'It's your life, isn't it?'

That was what she had told him over at the prairie-dog town. He dropped back and re-positioned his hat. 'Who would hire me; your brother?'

'Yes.'

'I don't think I should.'

'Why?'

'Well. I can think of several reasons.'

'Do it anyway, Mister Bronson.'

'. . . All right.'

She raised her face, it was faintly heat-flushed. 'Then we'd better start for home. It's mid-afternoon.'

He did not lift his hat nor move. 'No. You ride on alone. I'll come along later and hunt up your brother.'

She looked at his profile, as much as she could see of it beneath the hat. 'Why? Because you want the job on your own?'

'Yes'm. That's exactly why.' Now, he pushed the hat away and sat up. 'I want to say one more thing, then maybe you'll tell me not to ride on in for work.'

She sprang up. 'Then don't say it, Mister Bronson.' She grabbed her boots and ran out

39

where the horses were. He was awed at the way she could do that—barefoot.

CHAPTER FIVE

Compared to most cow outfits Senorio was not only larger, more solidly established but when Walter Bronson rode into the yard, it was like coming into a village.

The main-house was at the lower end of the wide, dusty yard, with a huge log barn on the left side, with the cookshack on the east side, and innumerable sheds for wagons, blacksmithing, storing food and so forth, scattered around. The bunkhouse, also of logs, was about twice the size of any bunkhouse Bronson had ever seen. It had two stovepipes, which meant it had a cook-stove inside as well as a wood-stove for heating.

The men were loafing in the late evening, after supper, some upon the cookshack porch, others over by the bunkhouse, and several more were at the barn. Frank Ballinger was at the tie-rack out front of the barn. He eyed Bronson before the younger man reached the yard, had sized him up, had guessed his reason for riding in, and nodded as Bronson reined toward the tie-rack. Frank had been in Marietta, as Jenny had predicted, but the mild euphoria he had brought out with him had been unable to survive the heavy meal he had recently eaten, so now he waited for the stranger to tie up saying nothing and looking as craggily authoritative as he usually looked.

Bronson said his name and offered a hand which Frank shook. Then Bronson mentioned work and Frank, who had been making his judgment all along, nodded solemnly. 'Yeah, we can use an extra hand. How are you with horses?'

Bronson smiled. 'Fair. Is that the job?'

Frank's answer showed caution. 'Maybe. We'll try you on the range for a few days.'

Bronson was willing. He had been through this before. Nor did he misjudge the craggy older man who had said his name was Frank Ballinger, and that he was Senorio's rangeboss—*segundo* to the Mexican cowboys. It was customary to try a new man at different jobs until he proved himself.

Frank said, 'Have you had supper?'

Benson nodded—he'd had one smashed sandwich; he was not hungry.

Ballinger gestured. 'The corrals are out back; turn your horse in and hang your rig on the pole in the barn, and take your saddlebags to any empty bunk you like over yonder.' Frank pushed up a tough smile. 'We don't work anyone to death, but we work 'em, Walter.' He turned, saw Beth and her brother come out to

41

the veranda at the main-house, and jutted his chin in that direction. 'Those are the owners. Barton and Beth Archer.'

Bronson looked, then reached to unloop the rein of his horse and lead it to the barn. An ancient Mexican the colour of old leather, watched Bronson, nodded and continued to watch. When Bronson slung his saddle over the pole he counted twelve saddles and the black-eyed old *vaquero* said, 'Ten riders, mister. It's a working cow outfit.'

Bronson took his animal out back, met two cowboys having a leisurely smoke back there leaning on corral stringers looking at the using stock. One was red-headed and had a peeling nose. He grinned and said his name was Mike Reilly. The other rider, darker, lean as a strip of rawhide, spat aside and also smiled. His name was Kenneth Hill. He had been on Senorio for seven years, was a tophand and was one of the men Frank Ballinger particularly depended on.

Walter Bronson told them who he was, that he had just been hired, and after watching his horse lie in the dust and roll, joined them at the corral fence where he rolled and lit a smoke.

Hill and Reilly were like most rangemen; they accepted anyone on sight, were easily cultivated and, like Frank Ballinger, would make their ultimate judgement slowly.

Later, most of the riders converged upon the lighted bunkhouse to resume a perpetual poker

42

session, but Walter Bronson remained down by the barn. Frank Ballinger, perhaps making a final round of the day, came upon Bronson down there, leaned and said, 'We run couple hundred head of horses over a hunnert and fifty thousand acres, and upwards of four thousand head of cattle.' Frank's knowledgeable eyes ranged over Bronson, not critically but not entirely un-critically either. 'It's an old outfit an' most of the men been here for quite a few years.' Frank gazed at his rough palm for a moment before going on. 'Some of us aren't gettin' any younger. You'll figure that out directly. Plenty of room on Senorio for good men who figure to stay.' He straightened up. 'There's a card game at the bunkhouse, if you've a mind to set in, Walter.'

Frank never got around to calling Bronson by the name the riders eventually labelled him by— Walt. But then Frank was still calling some of the oldest riders by their full first names, too.

It was the fourth day, with a light shower falling from a sky with only intermittent clouds, that Mike Reilly, Ken Hill and Walt Bronson waited out the passing shower among some oaks, and Mike summed up Frank Ballinger for Bronson's edification.

'He's been here all his best years. He's more protective about Senorio's interests than he'd be about his own. But Frank's a fair man. He's just gettin' old, and he's got some ideas from before we was born. Still, he's the *segundo* an' if he says jump, us fellers just ask how high.'

Reilly was easy-going, good natured, and typical in most ways of his variety of rangerider. Ken Hill on the other hand was more responsible, more capable of handling anything likely to crop up on the ranch, and less willing to evaluate the men he rode with—or—if he evaluated them, he did it privately.

All he said about old Frank was: 'Give him your best, Walt, and you got a friend for life. He may never show it, but that's how he's put together.'

The rain ended, they rode forth to continue their search for bulls which were off by themselves, and when they found two standing in a mud-bank along the upper reaches of Archer Creek, Walt sat his saddle with the other two, diagnosed the problem, and said, 'Is there anyone on the ranch who can make ox shoes?'

Ken Hill said shortly. 'Yeah, but Frank says if we got more'n enough bulls, a few can stand in the mud and it won't make much difference.'

Walt looked around. Ken was staring at the pair of stolid, one-ton redbacks, his face closed down against whatever his private thoughts were. Mike saw Walt's look, winked and shrugged thick shoulders.

They choused the bulls out of the creek-willows heading them in the direction of the last bunch of cows they had seen. Initially, the bulls

44

moved sluggishly, ponderously massive and stolidly unwilling. Then they caught the scent of cows and the rest of the push was easy.

The land was muggy after that shower. As the riders turned back to continue their search up along the creek, Ken Hill squinted disapprovingly at the spotty sky. 'Three baths I've had in the last ten days,' he said to no one in particular. 'Tonight'll be the fourth one. This damned sticky weather is a nuisance.'

But the grass did not seem to agree, it was flourishing. In places it was thick and matted enough to offer resistance to the passing horsemen. Walt was impressed by that. He did not especially enjoy muggy weather, but he was of the private opinion that in this life in order to get benefits, there also had to be sacrifices.

They got back to the home-place just ahead of dusk, barely in time to sluice off and slick down their hair before the cook beat his triangle for supper.

This night, Walt ate like a horse, listened to the teasing, the insults and sly innuendos which accompanied most cow-outfit suppers, and afterwards took his towel and soap and headed for Archer Creek a fair distance off to the west. By the time he had finished bathing several other men came out there for the same purpose, including Ken Hill.

One rider Walt had noticed, a stocky, greying, rather loquacious Texan, said, 'Who'n

45

hell was them fellers rode in as we was leaving?'

From the shadows farther along among the willows an accented voice answered. 'Sheriff Nolan from Marietta.'

The garrulous Texan hopped about tugging at a tight boot. 'Yeah? I didn't see 'em that close. What'n hell's he want out here?'

The same Mexican answered. '*Quien sabe?* You want me to guess? He is lookin' for Texans to deport.'

Laughter erupted elsewhere in the settling warm night. Walt grinned as he trudged back toward the lighted buildings. Behind him that loudmouthed Texan was insulting the *vaquero* in colourful terms.

The main-house was well-lighted. So was the bunkhouse. Across the yard there was a weaker light showing from the cookshack front windows, reflected in that direction from the *cosinero's* room off the kitchen.

There were a million stars without a single cloud to obscure them, and the steady warmth seemed unlikely to abate until along toward morning.

Walt ambled over to look in on his personal horse. The animal had paired off with a big mouse-coloured packmule, which amused Walt. He rolled and lit a smoke, savouring the peacefulness of the big ranch-yard in its insular setting of endless Senorio miles.

A soft voice over in the direction of the barn

behind him said, 'I looked all over.'

He turned, saw her framed as a pale silhouette in the black barn doorway, and killed his smoke before sauntering over.

She was wearing a dress. He had never seen her like that before. She looked regal; her stance was erect and lissom, her short dark hair was framed around the soft, golden contours of her face and she was not smiling when he came to halt and stand silently admiring her.

'You're beautiful,' he said softly.

She ignored it. 'Give me a direct yes or no answer. Have you ever been in a town called Mesquite?'

He nodded. 'In Colorado? Yes. Why?'

'Not in Colorado. In New Mexico. It's about a hundred and fifty miles east of here, on the spur-railroad. That's where we drive the cattle every autumn to ship them. Have you ever been there?'

'No, I never have,' he told her, beginning to lose some of the soft warmth he felt while gazing at her. 'Why?'

'Because the sheriff and two of his deputies are at the house with my brother asking if anyone on Senorio has seen a man they want for robbing a bank over there—and killing a cashier during the robbery.'

He waited a moment, then went still closer, until he could make out the white look on her face. 'Me . . . ?'

She had her hands clasped tightly across her stomach when she answered. 'The description is perfect, Mister Bronson.'

He stared at her. 'You think I'm a bank-robber?'

For a moment she simply looked at him. Then she answered. 'You came from the east. You told me that. You ride a big bay horse— with thoroughbred breeding . . .'

'Beth, there are more bay horses than any other colour. I came east from the stageroad where a sign said Marietta was on southward. I've never been a hundred and fifty miles farther east than that road. The description? I'm pretty average in build and all.'

She loosened her hands, turned slightly to look back up through the barn, then looked back, evidently having reached a conclusion. 'Ride, Mister Bronson,' she said softly and intently.

He answered curtly. 'Not on your life. I didn't rob any—'

'That won't matter,' she broke in almost harshly. 'They hang murderers. If you look like an outlaw, how can you prove you aren't him?' She looked around again, then back, and this time she leaned a little in her intensity. 'You came alone. Outside of me seeing you, who else has? They'll lock you up and if they never find the real outlaw, they'll try you.'

He listened, but did not really have to be

48

warned because he knew how rangeland justice worked as well as she did. And she was correct; he had come hundreds of miles by himself, had avoided towns and ranches because this was to be his loafing summer and he chose not to seek people, only new country in out-of-the-way places.

'Did you tell the sheriff about me?' he asked, and got a dark look along with a short answer. 'Of course not.' Then she said, 'But the men know you. So does Frank, and my brother told the sheriff he should go down to the bunkhouse after supper and talk to Frank. Mister Bronson—catch your horse and ride.'

He did not move. 'I told you—my name is Walter.'

She made an exasperated little hand-gesture. 'Walter ... Walter, go get your horse. I'll go back to the house and talk to Sheriff Nolan. I'll buy you as much time as possible, but please don't be long at rigging out and—'

'How do I get my bedroll and saddlebags from the bunkhouse? I can't just walk in, grab that stuff and walk out. Not with ten men staring at me.'

She paused, then swiftly said, 'Go up into the hills where you saw me when I fell. Stay out of sight up there. I'll wait until the men have ridden out in the morning, then get your things and bring them to you... Please—now go catch your horse!'

She turned on her heel and hurried back up through the barn leaving Walt Bronson standing out back having trouble digesting how swiftly and unexpectedly catastrophe had struck.

Then he turned and went after his horse.

Men hooting and laughing inside the bunkhouse made a pleasant sound as he brought in the horse to be rigged out. He was leading the horse out back when he heard someone coming across the dusty yard in the direction of the log barn. He swung up across leather and reined out on an angle so as to have the big old barn between himself and whoever was coming down there, until he could be far enough out for the darkness to hide him.

Then he reached the thick grass, booted his horse over into a leggy lope and kept him at it for almost a full hour, by which time he could no longer even see the lights of the Senorio buildings.

CHAPTER SIX

The instincts of a fugitive were in everyone. All that was required to bring them out was fear and pursuit. Walt did not develop the fear for a long time. Not until he was two-thirds of the way toward his destination in the hills, but the suspicion that there might be pursuit eventually encouraged the fear. By the time he was passing around that prairie-dog town where Beth had fallen, he was looking over his shoulder and occasionally stopping to listen.

But there was no pursuit. None that he could determine anyway, and in the moonless night unless lawmen knew where to go to seek a fugitive, they probably would not waste time groping aimlessly.

He thought of Beth, tried to fathom her ambivalent attitude. She had warned him, and that meant something—in fact it meant a great deal because otherwise those lawmen would have caught him without any effort.

He did not have to ask himself why she had done it. Since he'd poured the whiskey down her a week ago, out at the prairie-dog town, they had developed an easy, natural, yet unique relationship which, although he had not talked to her for four or five days afterwards, amounted to a special friendship.

Maybe it was more than that. As he reined toward the ghostly silhouette of the nearest foothills, he felt that it *was* more than that. He had thought of her often, particularly in the evenings when the day's work was done, and his recollection of her, the way she had appeared in the barn doorway, pale and beautifully feminine a few hours earlier, was a picture-memory he would carry in his mind and heart as long as he lived.

Otherwise, when he finally halted back where he'd made his last camp, despite the loss of his saddlebags and bedroll he would have kept on riding. Those things could be replaced. Anyway, it was summer, a man could get along fairly well without conveniences, at least until he located a town to buy replacements.

As he swung off and knelt to hobble the breedy big bay horse, he told himself he wanted the bedroll and saddlebags. He also told himself it was curiosity which made him compound the danger by waiting up here for her. But later, when the horse was grazing back where oaks and a few pines shielded the camp, and he was sitting with his back to a tree, he more correctly assessed his reason for not riding on—he wanted to see her again, even if it was for the last time.

He slept eventually, because it had been a long day, he was tired, and there was nothing else to do. But the pre-dawn chill roused him. He scouted for dry oak twigs and made a little fire. Dry oak gave off heat without smoke, but although he was thinking now as though he were a genuine fugitive, in this instance it was unnecessary; he could see all the open country below the foothill camp, out through the screen of trees which hid him from view, and there was no one in sight. In fact, excepting a band of horses to the west a fair distance, there was nothing to watch, not even any cattle.

The sun arrived, eventually, without much

heat for several hours, and its slow-growing soft brilliance further illuminated the miles of range country. Even those grazing horses were no longer in view.

He rubbed a hand over a lightly stubbled jaw, went out to remove his animal's hobbles, lead the animal to new feed and re-hobble it. He returned to the little fire, stoked it and hunkered in the warmth like a stoic old Indian squaw.

A long-tailed cougar came padding up into the hills after a nocturnal hunt out in the open country. He passed east through the trees and for some reason did not detect the smoke-scent, or, if he detected it did not heed it, and Walt watched his progress. He was a large male cat with scarred ears and a shiny hide. He was perhaps four or five years old, in his prime.

Walt could have shot him easily, and the idea crossed his mind. As a stockman he felt no compunction about this killing. Few animals could bring down a thousand pound cow, but this big cat could. Rangemen killed them on sight, along with wolves and bears, but this time Walt simply sat there watching.

Then the cat must have caught man-scent. With a startled swing of his head in Walt's direction, he bounded into the air and came down stretching for every inch of ground he could get over as he fled.

The bay horse did not see him, which was just

as well, for although he was hobbled and therefore could not flee, few things frightened a horse as badly as the sight, or the smell, of a big cat.

Walt let his little fire die to white ash as morning warmth arrived, and saw far-away movement to the southeast which he watched with rising expectations until, by the time he could be sure it was Beth Archer, a pleasant sensation spread through him.

She came directly to the foothills riding a black gelding whose easy gallop covered effortless miles right up to the moment she made him drop down to a slogging walk as she passed the prairie-dog town.

Walt watched the land beyond her. There was no other rider in sight. He walked down the slope to a small clearing and kept waving his hat until she saw him, then he turned back to the camp, and when she arrived later he greeted her with a broad smile which she returned, but not quite as widely.

He cared for her horse after she handed down his bedroll and saddlebags, then climbed off to say the Marietta lawman and his pair of hard-faced deputies had not left Senorio until this morning, having accepted her brother's offer to spend the night and have a decent breakfast before heading for town.

She walked out with him as he took her horse to feed, and as he knelt to buckle the hobbles

54

she said, 'The men were flabbergasted. They told Sheriff Nolan that if you were indeed an outlaw, you were the first one they had ever met who did not act in the least as though he thought the law might be looking for him. Ken Hill told the sheriff that if you were an outlaw he would eat his hat.'

Walt stood up, smiling at her. It was warming to hear these things, particularly since he had not been at Senorio for more than a few days longer than a week. He said, 'And you?'

She returned his steady look. 'I'm here, aren't I?'

They returned to the tree-hidden camp. He made a smoke and only looked up when she held out a bundle. 'Enough food to help out for a while,' she said.

He accepted the bundle. They stood looking straight at one another. 'Hell,' he said, forgetting to light the quirley, 'I don't want to leave, Beth.'

She let her eyes slide elsewhere. 'But you had better, Walter. Bob Nolan is a real manhunter. He's had that reputation for a long time.' She brought her gaze back. 'I don't want you to go, but I want you caught a whole lot less.'

She sank down in tree-shade looking as he had first seen her, in faded work trousers and a loose white blouse. Oddly, she still looked very feminine even in scuffed boots. He sank down nearby and a palpable silence endured between

55

them until he turned and caught her looking at him, then he said, 'Do you have doubts, Beth?'

She glanced at the shade a yard in front when she made a response 'No. I told myself last night when I came looking for you, that it was just not like you.' Her eyes swiftly rose to his face. 'Walter, what do I know about you?'

He said, 'Practically nothing.'

'But I *feel* something. I *feel* . . . this is a silly thing to say . . . I feel as though I knew you, had known you a long time.' She ruefully smiled at him. 'Female intuition. My brother says it's never right.'

He smiled. 'What does Jenny say?'

She was surprised, and laughed. Afterwards her body relaxed in the increasing, pleasant warmth. 'Jenny's told me at least a hundred times that the intuition women have is superior to anything men have.'

He continued to smile at her 'Then let's take Jenny's opinion. I like it better . . . As for feeling as though you've known me—that's not very strange because I've felt the same way since we first met at the pond.'

She watched his expression, his eyes and mouth, then pulled back from the edge of something else she felt, and became business-like. 'But you can't stay, Walt. Bob Nolan knows you were on the ranch. He thinks you saw their badges last night which was why you ran. But he's a manhunter; he'll start a search.'

56

For Bronson the logic of her statement was valid, but he was still indignant about having to flee from something he had known nothing about until she had told him last night; something he had never done, had never even contemplated doing, and most certainly had not done in a town named Mesquite which he had never visited.

There was also another reason but he did not mention it. Perhaps he did not have to; she may have guessed more about his reasons for being reluctant than he suspected because she said, 'And come back . . . someday.'

He tossed his hat aside in the grass. He had learned early in life the value of being patient. But right now he was having trouble about that. 'Someday could be a long while.'

'A long while, Walt, is better than never,' she said softly.

He understood the implication and looked over at her. 'If this manhunting sheriff is such a successful lawman . . .'

She smiled a little. 'In time he'll find the real outlaw.'

'Will he?'

She nodded. 'I have confidence in Bob Nolan. Everyone does in this country.'

Walt got comfortable in the shade, lying half-facing her. He said, 'Hadn't you better go back?'

Her answer came slowly. 'No. I was careful to

ride due west for a long while just in case anyone was watching, which I'm sure they weren't. Then I turned up in this direction and didn't see a soul. But the crew is split up today: some of the men are probably riding the lower foothills to turn back strays, and if I rode down out of here in full daylight they'd probably see me.'

He kept looking at her. It had sounded to him as though she did not intend to leave until dusk. She reddened slightly and jumped up. 'You haven't eaten. I'll be right back.'

He twisted to watch her go back where the saddle had been up-ended and kneel to rummage in a saddle-bag. When she was striding back he sighed and sank down in the upland short-grass. The sky was clear and softly blue. He would come back; with a woman like that waiting, he'd come back if he had to battle his way through an army of manhunting lawmen.

She had coarse sourdough bread, a flask of coffee which was still hot, and a bottle which held fried beans and steak. She even had a plate for him, something he had not owned in ten years, and a fork. As she handed him the coffee she smiled. He wagged his head. 'You're a special person,' he told her. 'Do you realise what would probably happen if your friend the manhuntin' sheriff was to ride in here right now and find you with me?'

She finished with the plate and put it in front

of him. 'No one's going to ride in here. Eat.'

He did, not as hungry now as he had been earlier. Her presence undoubtedly had something to do with that. But he ate; he would have eaten in any case after all the trouble she had gone to for him.

Later, she followed him to a trickling seepage-spring while he stripped to the waist, scrubbed, then propped up his steel mirror from the saddlebags and shaved. She talked; about nothing in particular; about her parents, her earlier years, the death of her mother, then of her father, of Barton and Senorio. When he was finished and had splashed water over his shaved face, she handed him his saddle-bag towel with a tart comment.

'If that towel's been washed in the past six months I'll be surprised.'

He considered his towel. It was small, frayed, and had a perpetually greyish tinge. 'I washed it last month in central Colorado,' he said reproachfully. 'Maybe it don't *look* clean, but it is.'

Her eyes twinkled. 'Bury it and I'll bring you another one.'

Their eyes met and held. He understood the implication behind her words. Then she seemed to regret that moment of softness and said, '*Someday* I'll bring you another one. Today, after I leave, you've got to ride on.' She turned to avoid his gaze, and pointed. 'There is nothing

59

west of here for more than two hundred miles. If you stay in the foothills no one will see you. Fifty or so miles onward where the hills get brushy and rocky, you can come down into open country. There won't be any riders that far out.' Her hand fell back to her lap. 'There's a town called Vicksburg . . .'

He was looking steadily at her. When their eyes met, and held, his gaze disconcerted her, scattering her thoughts. He said, 'Beth, I don't want to leave you.'

Her answer was quiet and candid. 'I don't want you to leave . . . me.'

It was cool and shady there by the seepage spring. There were also a million mosquitoes so they went back to the camp. On the way her fingers sought his hand, closed around it, and when he squeezed, she returned the squeeze.

That small physical contact destroyed the fragile barrier which had been between them up to this point. When they walked past the grazing horses and he halted to look at the animals, bringing her around, she suddenly went up against him, dug her face into his chest and did not say a word.

He brought up both arms to hold her. His heart suddenly increased its tempo; he was sure she could feel the solid beat. After a moment of prickly uncertainty he leaned, kissed her cheek, felt her straightening up and when her face lifted, his mouth felt for hers.

It was not a passionate kiss, not that time, it was sweet and gentle—and uncertain. Afterwards neither of them said a word as they pulled back and continued on over to the camp.

CHAPTER SEVEN

She left with the beginning of early dusk. He watched her ride down out of the hills and out across the open range with a tumult of emotions which he could not have sorted out and re-ordered if he had tried.

Then he turned heavily back to strike his camp, to roll the bedroll and re-pack the saddlebags which he had unpacked that morning to shave. Finally, as he stood in the fading day looking out where she had disappeared, he felt more depressed than he could recall ever having felt before, and for something to do with his hands, rolled a smoke.

There was no particular hurry so he leaned against a tree thinking back to the moments following the one when they had first touched. He had never experienced anything like that before, and right at this moment he did not believe it would be possible for him to ever feel that way again. He was right; between a man and a woman it only happened that way, once.

He dropped the quirley, ground it underfoot,

picked up a rope and went after his horse. The animal seemed willing to leave. He was not a particularly restless horse, but as with all thoroughbreds or half-thoroughbreds, when he was rested and as full as a tick, he was willing to move out.

Walt did not work fast. The reluctance to leave this country was stronger now than it had been when Beth had first appeared. He had the saddle in place, cinched up, and was lashing the saddlebags along with the bundle she had brought him to the skirts behind the cantle when his horse turned its head, ears alertly pointed. Walt had one moment to feel a premonition pushing up through the other emotions, then a man quietly spoke from up through the northward trees, his voice calm and as cold as ice.

'Come around on the north side of the horse, and don't do anything rash, mister.'

Walt's surprise was so complete he leaned across the saddle, staring. The stranger was visible as a continuation of dusk and shadows where he was standing with a carbine pointed, being held across his body with both hands. Walt could not see the hammer but he knew without seeing it that the man over yonder had it pulled all the way back for instant firing.

'Mister,' the calm, cold voice said, 'come around on my side of the horse.'

Walt still hung there, but now the

astonishment was past. He turned to obey thinking to himself that Beth had been absolutely correct about her friend the lawman from Marietta.

When he was in full view the lawman gave his second command. 'Shuck that belt-gun . . . carefully, mister.'

Walt obeyed, let the sixgun fall to the grass at his feet, and waited.

The grizzled, deeply tanned man let his carbine barrel droop a little and strolled down out of the trees to halt directly in front of Walt. The badge which had not been visible before was clearly so now. They stood looking at one another until the sheriff finally grounded his saddlegun and leaned a little on it.

'That bedroll,' he said, jutting his chin in the direction of the laden horse behind Walt, 'and those saddlebags—they were at the Senorio bunkhouse last night, mister, after you fled . . . Who brought them to you today?'

Walt sighed inwardly. If the sheriff did not know that, then he had not seen Beth either coming out here or going back. Walt made no attempt to reply.

The lawman was spare, faded and not quite as old as Frank Ballinger, but a lot older than Walt was. He possessed a granite jaw and smoky eyes which reminded Walt of a reptile the way they never seemed to blink. If appearances meant anything, this man was everything Beth had

63

warned Walt that he was.

Nolan considered the silence after asking his questions, and said, 'What's your name?'

Walt told him. 'Bronson. Walter Bronson.'

'I'm Sheriff Nolan from Marietta. You saw me last night in the Senorio yard.'

It would do no good to deny that he had ever put eyes upon Sheriff Nolan before so Walt continued to be silent. Nolan shook his head a little. He seemed to have completed his study of Walt Bronson.

'That wasn't very damned smart, Bronson, stopping over here to get a job. If I'd been in your boots I wouldn't have even slowed down until I was five hundred miles from Mesquite.'

Walt shifted stance putting all his weight on his left leg. He had no intention of volunteering anything, and right now he was perfectly willing for Sheriff Nolan to going on being garrulous; it gave Walt time to make some decisions and to think of plausibilities.

Nolan said, 'Who was it, Bronson? You know what I mean. Who packed your gatherings out to you?'

Walt remained obdurately silent. Nolan considered the strong features in front of him, then seemed to give it up because when next he spoke he said, 'You must be a flat-lander. Any time you're in the hills, Bronson, don't stop in the lower ones because anyone who is lookin' for you will go to the highest ground where they can see all movement down below.'

Walt's respect for this craggy-looking older man rose a notch. 'That's what you did, Sheriff?'

'Yeah ... But there's more to it.'

Walt had a sudden stab of worry. 'What else?'

'In open country a man don't stay out where folks can see him.' Nolan looked past at the bay horse, who was now standing hipshot with his lower lip hanging, dozing in the warm evening. 'I think that horse could have left me far behind, if it'd come down to a horse race. Where did you get him—out of someone's pasture on a dark night?'

Walt smiled despite the heat of raw anger which boiled up in him. No one liked being called a horsethief, not even horsethieves.

'I bought him as a three-year-old on a cow outfit in southern Wyoming. That was four years ago. He's branded on the left shoulder if you want to look it up and write the ranch.'

Having said that much, Walt wanted to say more, but Sheriff Nolan was unwilling. He had finished what he had started out to do, the moment he discovered that someone had removed Bronson's personal property from the Senorio bunkhouse *after* the ranch-hands had been told Bronson was a fugitive.

All Nolan wanted now was to get back to Marietta with his captive, and while there was still sufficient light to see by, he also wanted to get his prisoner down into the open country, so he gestured with the carbine-barrel.

'Get on your horse and ride north at a walk, ahead of me.'

Walt obeyed, surmising, correctly, that Sheriff Nolan had left his saddle-animal back up among the northward pines. He drew rein and watched his captor sidle around, walk back a yard or two to free a tethered saddlehorse, then swing up, all without once taking his eyes off Bronson.

As they turned back southward, Sheriff Nolan in the rear, Walt said, 'You've heard this a lot of times, Sheriff . . . I didn't rob a bank nor shoot anyone.'

'No? Then why did you run last night when me and my deputies rode in? Unless you had known about that robbery an' killing, Bronson, you wouldn't have had any reason to run. Innocent men don't run when they see lawman approaching.'

Walt lapsed back into silence. He could not explain how he had known there was a robbery and murder without revealing *how* he had known. Nor could he explain why he had fled without being equally candid. The fact that Nolan had not seen Beth made it obligatory that Walt say nothing.

They reached open country, Nolan growled for Walt to turn east in the direction of the stageroad, and parallel to the foothills which were now on their left side. Clearly, Nolan, for all his obvious conviction that someone from the Senorio home-place had aided the fugitive, did not intend to ride back down to the ranch tonight.

Walt looped his reins and built a smoke. As he lit up he wagged his head. If he and Beth had not... Well; if that was the price for this long, fragrant and wonderful day together, it was worth every bit of it—and more.

Nolan loosened a little when they had the stageroad in sight. He cocked his head at the new moon which was belatedly rising, guessed the time and said, 'Turn south when you reach the road... And Bronson; I'll find the feller who brought your gatherings out to you. I'll have him in the same cell with you by tomorrow night.'

Walt started to turn up onto the verge of the roadway as he answered Nolan's boast. 'I'll bet you ten dollars you don't.'

Nolan answered curtly and with spirit. 'It's a bet... Do you have ten dollars?'

'Yeah. But that's all I have.'

'Where did you cache that bag of money from the bank?'

Walt halted, waited until Nolan was beside him, then turned to answer. 'Sheriff; I didn't rob that bank. I've never been in Mesquite, New Mexico Territory, in my life.' He paused and at the look he was getting, added a little more. 'I hope to hell the law over in Mesquite does a better job of running down the real outlaw than you've done.'

Sheriff Nolan's retort was cool. 'Bronson, I've got a nice adobe jailhouse which is never hot inside no matter how hot it gets outside. You'll get fed twice a day, and you'll rot there until you tell me the details of that killin' and robbery.'

They rode down the star-washed warm night until, with town-lights ahead, Sheriff Nolan made a smoke, inhaled, exhaled, and when they were in the outskirts, said, 'Except for that murder, if you gave back the money you might have got off easier. As for the cache; I got two deputies ridin' for me who can read sign in a rainstorm. They'll back-track you.'

Walt stubbed out his smoke atop the saddlehorn. There was no point in keeping a conversation alive between them. He gazed ahead at the town of Marietta with cautious interest. By starlight it looked pleasant enough, with tree-lined roads and several spur-roads off the main thoroughfare which also had stores. Marietta supplied a very large segment of the plateau countryside. It had a distinction no other Western cowtown could equal. It had been the site of the farthest-west battle between Union and Confederate forces during the Civil War when a gold-starved Confederacy had sent a column of soldiers overland in a desperate bid to reach and plunder the California goldfields.

At Marietta the Confederacy's hopes were smashed when Union horse-soldiers had decisively beaten and routed the Confederates.

It was an old town compared to most cow-country towns, and it clearly showed its Mexican heritage. Most of the buildings were, like Bob Nolan's jailhouse, made of massively thick adobe bricks, one wall built against a first and second wall.

The jailhouse, where Nolan herded in his prisoner, had steel bars embedded into those massive walls, and since this did not appear to be a later addition, after the United States had acquired New Mexico—all the Southwest—the jailhouse must have also served in that capacity for the former rulers of the country. In those days it had been called a *calabozo*.

Nolan lighted a lamp in his office, had Walt empty his pockets into his hat, then motioned for Walt to go along the wall to a bench and be seated while Sheriff Nolan pawed through the hat. When he finished he looked up. 'Don't you own anything with your name on it, Bronson?'

As a matter of fact Walt didn't. He had no family left. He had written to no one in many years and therefore had received no letters. Nor was it uncommon for rangemen to be without identification, and as Walt saw this now, it was not important.

'No,' he answered. 'What difference does it make? You've got your mind made up.'

Nolan stuffed the hat and its contents into a lower desk-drawer and leaned back in his chair studying the prisoner. 'What's your story? You're just a drifting rangerider?'

Walt had to smile. 'That's exactly what I am.'

Nolan nodded. 'Sure. And you've been riding the back-trails so no one saw you.'

Walt's smile faded a little. 'Just lock me up,' he said. 'I'm tired. And right now I don't feel like visiting.'

Nolan teetered on his chair for a moment, then shot up to his feet fishing in a pocket for a key. 'Just once I'd like to hear one of you fellers come up with a new story.'

The cell-room was warm with high, recessed, very narrow windows in the walls above a man's head, but if they had been two feet lower it would not have offered much encouragement to prisoners; they were not only heavily barred, they were also too narrow for a man to squeeze through.

As Nolan locked the door from the outside he said, 'It might help if you told me where the cache is. It likely wouldn't help a hell of a lot . . . Those folks over in Mesquite are mad as hell over that cold-blooded shooting, but people with money in banks get over that kind of anger after a few weeks, and begin to think about their money.'

Walt turned from inspecting the cell. There was absolutely nothing he could say to Sheriff

70

Nolan which the lawman would believe, or which would help Walt.

He crossed to the barred door and looked at Nolan. 'What time do you fetch breakfast, Sheriff?'

Nolan turned on his heel.

Walt went to the bunk with its straw-filled mattress and sat down. Until an hour or so earlier he had not come to the full realisation of his predicament, so now he sat in gloom thinking about it, and the longer he sat there the more hopeless it looked. Unless someone, perhaps the authorities over in that town which had been robbed, could come up with the actual bandit.

He sighed, leaned his shoulders against the wall and pushed out his legs. In a country where distances were vast, towns few and far between, and where fleeing fugitives, once they got clear of the town they had raided, usually resembled every other rangerider, an awful lot of outlaws survived uncaught. In fact throughout the western cow country banditry could hardly have flourished as it did unless the circumstances which surrounded it were so amenable to success, and Walt, like everyone else, was very aware of this. But until he was locked into the Marietta jailhouse none of this had ever seemed likely to involve him.

71

CHAPTER EIGHT

Sheriff Nolan was in no hurry. He fed his prisoner in the morning without a word passing between them, then he went back to the cafe with his pair of deputies for a leisurely breakfast with considerable talk between mouthfuls. He was convinced he had the Marietta raider and to acquire proof he told his deputies where he had collared Bronson, and instructed them to back-track him.

The hawk-faced fair-haired deputy who was the tracker, scowled. 'How?' he demanded. 'That feller's been on Senorio for dang near two weeks. How the hell do we find tracks that are two weeks old when we don't even know which direction he came from?'

Nolan had already considered this. 'Take Ballow's hound.'

The hawk-faced deputy leaned back holding a coffee cup. 'There was a light rain a few da؟ back, Bob.' Then he seemed ready to yield. 'All right. We'll do our best. But don't build up your hopes.' The two deputies exchanged a look when Sheriff Nolan lowered his head. The deputy who had been sitting there listening, raised and lowered his shoulders.

Later, Sheriff Nolan went to visit the bear-hunter who owned the hound dog, a grizzled bachelor named Carter Ballow. The agreement was made; for two-bits a day the deputies could take the hunting hound, but if anything happened to his dog Carter Ballow wanted an even fifty dollars. Nolan agreed, but on the way back to his office he cursed under his breath. A man could buy a sound, strong, young, broke saddle horse for fifty dollars.

Sheriff Nolan had no knowledge of how rare a dog was who could track both big game animals, and men, entirely by scent.

Later, he got his horse from the liverybarn and rode out of town in the direction of the Senorio home-place. He did not expect the riding crew to be there, but at this point he was not worried because only he and his two deputies knew he had captured Walter Bronson. The Senorio rider who had aided Bronson would have no reason to be worried.

When he reached the yard the cook was out behind his kitchen doing a wash and did not know anyone had ridden in until he heard two men call greetings back and forth over in front of the barn. Out of curiosity the cook went to the corner of the cookshack in time to see Sheriff Nolan dismount across the yard where Barton Archer was standing.

For Barton, the visit was a surprise. After yesterday he had not expected to see Sheriff Nolan again so soon, but as Nolan was looping his reins, he cleared that up with one sentence.

'I got him last night, about dusk, Bart. He was saddling up to head out.'

'Where was he?' asked the rancher.

Nolan gestured. 'Up yonder in the foothills northwest of here. Up across your horse range.'

Barton frowned. 'That wasn't very far considering how much time he had to be a lot farther along.'

'Well; he left here so sudden that his gatherings were still in the bunkhouse... He was waitin' up there until someone brought them to him.'

Barton Archer's scowl deepened. 'From here, Bob?'

Sheriff Nolan gravely inclined his head, and leaned on the rack looking at Archer. 'Yeah, from here. When I caught him he was tying the bedroll and saddlebags on his horse, along with a bundle of grub wrapped in a blue cloth; it looked to me like a real small tablecloth or a hell of a big napkin ... I didn't see who brought that stuff to him. Maybe I should have; I was ridin' the higher country watchin' as I rode, but mainly I was watchin' the lower sidehills. Anyway, that's why I rode out today. Would Frank know who was absent yesterday?'

Barton Archer considered the ground for a moment, then said, 'Bob, Frank usually splits the crew. Some go one way, some go another way.' He looked up. 'If one of them slipped back here, unless Beth or I saw him, or the cook, he could have taken those things from the bunkhouse, delivered them to Bronson, and providing none of the other men saw him doing that, he would be able to do it safely.'

Sheriff Nolan gazed across at the cookshack, then faced Archer again. 'You mind if I talk to the cook and your sister?'

'No, I don't mind. But Beth's on the range somewhere. Usually, she doesn't get back much before the men do. But you're plumb welcome to wait... I've got to go over to the Marietta range for a while, but I'll be back before sundown.'

Bob Nolan led his horse into the barn to stall it, and when he returned to the yard Barton Archer threw him a high wave as he cantered out of the yard.

Nolan strolled over to the cookshack, heard noise out back and walked around where the bull-necked, barrel-chested older man was vigorously scrubbing grey towels upon a washboard. The cook looked around, eyed Sheriff Nolan without smiling or nodding, then withdrew thick hands and arms from the scrub-bucket and dried them on a limp cloth as he said, 'Howdy.'

Nolan knew the cook, a former freighter and a rangeman who had broken a hip in an accident years earlier and since then had been unable to do the things he had formerly done. His name was Al Strickland. Nolan had upon several

75

occasions had to jail Strickland for being drunk and troublesome in town, but there had never been any particular animosity over those interludes.

The cook stepped back into overhang shade along the rear of the building and said, 'Surprised the hell out of me about that cowboy bein' a bank-robber.'

Nolan also got into the shade. 'He wasn't a very smart one or he would have left the country.'

Strickland's eyes widened. 'Didn't he?'

'Nope. I nailed him last night in the foothills above the Senorio horse pasture.'

'What in hell was he waitin' for?'

Sheriff Nolan fished forth his tobacco sack and went to work making a smoke. 'Someone from here took his bedroll and saddlebags to him.' Nolan offered the sack but the cook shook his head and stared.

'From here? You mean, one of the other fellers . . . ?'

Nolan lit up. 'Yeah. Al, by any chance did you see someone come back to the yard yesterday, then ride out again?'

Strickland fished out a limp bandana and re-dried his hands and thought. Then he said, 'Yestiddy I spent the mornin' huskin peas and black-eyed beans for a stew. I was out back here where it's usually cooler than out front. Nope, I didn't even hear anyone. And yestiddy afternoon I was in the yard for a while but no one come back. In fact no one come in at all until the regular time when they all come driftin' back.' As the lawman was unhappily considering his cigarette the cook remembered something. 'I see Miss Archer go out pretty early, but she was a long way off before I knew who it was—she had the barn between me and her.'

Sheriff Nolan passed over that. 'One of them,' he said quietly, more to himself than to the *cosinero*. 'They still got ten hired riders, Al?'

'Yeah. But you could eliminate Manuelito. He's ailin' and don't hardly ever ride out no more. He stays pretty much to his little shack over by the wagon-shed.'

With a hint of hope in his voice Nolan said, 'Maybe I'd ought to go talk to him.'

Strickland's response was immediate. 'Naw. You'd be wastin' your time. Old Manuelito can't see from here to that wash-tub any more, and you got to dang near yell to have him hear you. A whole blessed troop of cavalry could charge through the yard with bugles blowin' and ol' Manuelito wouldn't see nor hear 'em.'

For a while they leaned in the shade without speaking. Nolan was not dismayed, not yet; he had the balance of the day ahead, and in his experience as a lawman things like this were only very rarely resolved easily or quickly. He and the cook went indoors for a cup of coffee

77

and a bowl of the best chili Bob Nolan had ever eaten. He smiled at Strickland, which was something he seldom did, and paid the cook a compliment.

'Best damned beans in the Territory.'

Strickland was in fact not only a good cook, but he was also an innovative one, two attributes not very many cow-camp cooks possessed. He was also an even-tempered man, as a rule, and was liked by the riders. At one time he had been a man of great physical power. He had used it upon occasion, but Strickland was not an individual who carried grudges. Now, watching Sheriff Nolan spoon in chili, he said, 'Maybe that feller snuck back here hisself, and got his gatherings.'

Nolan looked up briefly. 'Maybe. Only if he did that—why in hell was he loafin' around in the hills when he knew damned well I'd be after him?'

Strickland leaned on the table thinking, finally he said, 'Yeah, you're right. He wouldn't be hangin' around he'd be splittin' the wind gettin' a long way from here . . . More chili?'

'If it's all right.'

The cook arose, limped to the pot, refilled the bowl and returned with it. As he sat down he said, 'Hell, Sheriff, that feller wasn't on the ranch but maybe a week or ten days. Folks don't usually cotton to other folks that fast. Not cotton to 'em enough to risk trouble with the

78

law about 'em.'

Nolan's reply to that was short. '*Someone* cottoned to him that much.' He finished his second bowl of chili and sat back, replete. 'When the riders drift in, don't mention any of this to them. I don't want another feller to bust out of here in the night.'

Strickland was agreeable, and Sheriff Nolan ambled back to the yard where he encountered the ailing old Senorio horse-breaker. Manuelito was aiming for a log bench out front of the barn where the late day sun did not reach directly, but where heat stored in the front-wall logs continued to seep out, into a man's back, all afternoon.

Nolan had known Manuelito since he had first come to the Marietta countryside, and as he approached the old man now he did not believe Manuelito looked much different, except that he was more stooped.

Manuelito peered with a quizzical stare until he recognised Nolan, then he slapped the bench at his side and said '*Sentarse,*' as he patted the bench with a mahogany hand. 'They told me about the *pistolero*. Did you catch him?'

'Yeah, I caught him last evening in the hills above the horse pasture.'

The old Mexican said, 'A-hah!' Then he sat a moment before turning to peer at Sheriff Nolan. 'No farther than that?'

Nolan sighed. He was tiring of these

79

questions, and his same answers. 'Yeah. He waited up there.'

Manuelito's rheumy eyes brightened a little. 'Waited? Waited for someone from here?'

'Yeah.'

'Who, then?'

'I don't know. That's why I'm back out here today, *viejo*. Someone took his bedroll and saddlebags up to him. He was waiting for them, and the other rider knew where to find the outlaw.'

Manuelito continued to sit for a long while staring at Sheriff Nolan. Gradually, then, he eased back to face forward and sat like a mahogany gnome. Eventually he said, 'That would have been in the morning, then, *amigo*.'

'Yes.'

'But not too early, because the other men were in sight around the range. And not too late because that's a long ride up there.'

Bob Nolan leaned back with his shoulders against the warm log wall. 'Yeah. Something like that.'

Manuelito lapsed back into his silence, and shifted slightly on the bench because it was of unyielding wood and he no longer possessed the padding for sitting he had once possessed.

Slowly, Nolan's perceptive hunch went to work. The Sheriff turned. 'Who did you see, Manuelito?'

'I didn't say I saw anyone,' the old horseman

replied.

Nolan continued to stare at the wizened old man's profile. 'But you were out back.'

'Well, yes, I was back there.'

'And you saw a rider?'

Manuelito's age and infirmities did not seem to affect his reasoning processes. 'Anyone can tell you, Sheriff, I don't see as well as I once did. And the sun was in my eyes as well.'

Nolan leaned off the log wall. 'But you saw him ride out?'

'I see them all ride out. Sometimes. Some mornings I don't get up that early. Some mornings I don't feel good so I stay in my bunk until—'

'Manuelito, it was after the riders had gone. Maybe an hour or so afterwards, wasn't it?'

The old man shrugged thin shoulders. 'Who knows what the time was?'

'But it was after the other men had gone.'

'Yes. After that.'

'Exactly what could you make out, Manuelito?'

'...*Madre de Dios*!' exclaimed the old man in a fit of sudden exasperation. 'I told you—I don't see very well any more... It was someone on a black horse, but his back was to me and there was the sun. That's all I know, may God strike me dead if it isn't.'

Nolan rolled and lit a smoke, then handed it to the old man, changed the subject and got the old horse-breaker to recalling things from his past. After an hour of this, with the sun sinking, old Manuelito had nearly forgotten their earlier conversation. He was a very old man, he himself did not know how old, he had lived a full and colourful life. He told stories to Nolan until three riders coming in from the northeast caught Nolan's attention. One was Barton Archer, one was Frank Ballinger the *segundo*, and the third man was that lanky, somewhat dark-looking rider named Hill. Ken Hill.

Sheriff Nolan patted Manuelito on the shoulder, arose and sauntered to the front of the barn to await the oncoming riders. He had just one question for Frank. When he got the answer to that, he would still be able to take a new prisoner back to Marietta this evening—and collect that ten dollars from Walter Bronson.

CHAPTER NINE

Barton excused himself to go up to the main-house, which was entirely agreeable with Sheriff Nolan. And when the taciturn tophand, Ken Hill, took his horse and the other two animals into the barn to care for them, that too was agreeable with Nolan.

He and Frank were out front by the tie-rack. Old Manuelito went shuffling off in the direction of the cookshack and Frank gravely watched this as Sheriff Nolan explained his reason for being back at Senorio today, something which Barton had already confided in Frank, so Ballinger turned from watching Manuelito and said, 'Yeah, I know. Bart already asked me who could have snuck back yesterday and hauled Bronson's stuff up to him.' Frank paused, gazing steadily at the lawman. 'I sent the men north to push back any drift into the hills. That took three of them. I sent another three to the south range, and the rest of us rode the Marietta range.'

Nolan did not play his trump card just yet. He instead asked if any of the men could have cut back and Frank shrugged. 'Not the fellers who rode with me, Bob. We stayed together all day. Maybe one of the other fellers could have, I don't know. But you can ask around if you've a mind to.'

Perhaps the reason why Frank Ballinger and Bob Nolan were not good friends after all the years they had known each other was because they were very much alike. Neither smiled readily nor often, both were totally practical, tough men with no illusions, and in this particular case Frank viewed the lawman's visit to Senorio as a kind of reflection against the outfit. There was nothing in his life which mattered as much to the *segundo* as Senorio. He did not even tolerate half-joking, sly, adverse remarks among the men who rode for the outfit, so now he stood gazing at Sheriff Nolan from an expressionless face which showed nothing at all except his dislike.

Bob Nolan understood exactly. He admired Frank's loyalty; he admired loyalty in anyone, even in the men he occasionally hunted down. But he too was loyal—to the law. 'Did any of the fellers ridin' with you yesterday,' he said, 'ride a black horse?'

Frank thought a moment, then slowly shook his head, but as he turned slightly to glance out where other riders were crossing toward the yard from the east, Bob Nolan saw a sudden shadowy spasm cross the rangeboss's features. It came and went in a second. Frank turned back and said. 'No. There was bays and greys. You figure this feller rode a black horse?'

Nolan too eyed the incoming rangeriders. 'Yeah.'

Frank's response was predictable. 'Maybe it was a seal-brown, Sheriff.'

Nolan knew better. Manuelito was a horseman; a cowboy too, but primarily a horseman and horsemen never made that mistake. 'Black,' he retorted, bringing his gaze back to Frank after having ascertained that none of the incoming riders was straddling a black horse.

Frank straightened up off the tie-rack. 'If you want I'll find out which one it was—ridin' a

84

black horse.'

Nolan studied old Frank. 'That'll be fine. The main thing Frank, is that I don't want him spooked. If he lights out it'll be dark before I can overhaul him.'

'If I find him, Sheriff, he won't leave. I promise you that.'

Ballinger walked tiredly in the direction of the barn and Sheriff Nolan went over to the log bench so the incoming riders could use the tie-rack without having someone leaning there.

The sun was nearly gone but daylight would linger for some time yet. As those four men at the rack were tying up another rider loped toward the yard from the southeast. Sheriff Nolan studied the big sorrel horse for a moment before he recognised Beth Archer. He watched her approach the same way any healthy man would have watched, but not for long. He left the front of the barn as she came in, to go out back and look at the corralled horses.

There was probably a black horse among the animals which had not been used today, or which had recently been used and had been turned in with the other horses.

Beth had not recognised Sheriff Nolan on the ride in, nor did she hear the men mention his presence as she cared for her horse, and stalled it in the barn because she intended to use the same horse the following day.

She met Ken Hill leaning on the barn-front

on her way across the yard, and thought he looked more reticent than usual, but because she was hungry she headed unerringly for the main-house.

Her brother was sitting in the shadows up there on the veranda with a glass of watered whiskey in one hand. He watched her approach and when she smiled and came up the steps he did not smile back. He pointed to a vacant chair and said, 'I want to talk to you, Beth.'

His tone was grave and his gaze was hard. She halted, studying him, then went obediently to the chair. 'Is it trouble?' she asked.

He offered the glass. She declined and faintly frowned. Rarely had they ever argued but he seemed ready to argue now. At least he was cool toward her as he pulled back the glass, drank half its contents, then turned his head so that he was staring directly at her when he spoke.

'Sheriff Nolan's down around the barn.'

That surprised her. She had not seen him. It also, for some reason, gave her a sudden sinking sensation.

'He caught Bronson last night in the hills north of the horse pasture.'

She fought to keep from raising a hand to her throat. Barton was watching every move, every hint of an expression. He had deliberately surprised her that way because he wanted to see her reaction. He had seen it, so now he drained the glass and set it beside his chair upon the porch floor.

'Someone took Bronson's bedroll and saddlebags to him yesterday. From here.'

She concentrated on keeping her face perfectly calm. Inside, she was in tumult.

Barton said, 'Beth, Nolan told me that when he caught Bronson, he not only had his bedroll and saddlebags, but he also had a bundle of grub in a blue cloth...' Barton let that lie between them for a moment. 'While I was out today that kept bothering me. When I got back a half hour or so ago, I went to the pantry and had Jenny lay out her blue tablecloth and napkins... Nolan thinks it was one of the *men* who met Bronson yesterday. We know better, don't we?'

She sat like stone without answering.

'Beth, one of the blue napkins is missing. If it *had* been one of the rangemen, they couldn't have got hold of that blue napkin Nolan has at the jailhouse in Marietta, but I don't believe I have to see it. Do I?' He sat gazing at her through a long interlude of silence. When she still said nothing, Barton said, 'Why? Why in the hell did you help an outlaw—a murderer?'

That broke the spell for her. 'He's no more a murderer than you are, Bart, or than I am.'

'Because he told you he wasn't? You talk to this man once and now you know him so well that—?'

'Bart, I knew him before he hired on. I was the one who asked him to talk to Frank about a job. When I was up looking at the broodmares my horse fell with me. He came along and helped me... We went over to the Piney Woods... we spent that whole day together...'

Barton did not move. He seemed to be digesting all this with some kind of premonition, and while he was normally an almost imperturbably calm, assured individual, this had caught him totally unprepared.

'I was the one who warned him the other night when Sheriff Nolan came looking for that robber and killer.' Beth felt breathless so she waited a moment before continuing. 'You don't know him. He's no killer, Bart.'

Finally, her brother ordered his thoughts, and spoke. 'What you are implying—at least that's how it seems to me—is that you and this cowboy are very close friends, Beth. What in gawd's name were you thinking of when you helped him? If he isn't the man Bob Nolan's after, he didn't have to run and you didn't have to put yourself in his same category by helping him. Nolan ... Beth, do you realise that Nolan will figure all this out eventually? Then what? ... Damn! I don't believe you thought this through. I don't think you realise what you've done... You've put yourself in the position of being an accomplice to a robber and a killer.'

She jumped up. 'Walt Bronson is neither one!'

'Why? Because he told you he wasn't?'

Barton, who swore only occasionally and even then never very violently, also sprang up. 'For Christ's sake, Beth, you're not going to be able to keep this from Nolan.' At the sound of boots crossing through the settling dusk toward the veranda, Barton turned slightly. It was Frank Ballinger. The *segundo* saw Beth up there, hesitated a step, then came on, removing his hat as he stalked heavily up the stairs and turned, facing Barton.

'I'd like a word with you alone, Barton,' Balllinger said, unwilling to meet Beth's stare.

She did not give her brother an opportunity to speak. 'What is it, Frank? Does it have something to do with Walt Bronson?'

Frank turned hard, pale eyes upon her. 'Yes'm. And not just Bronson. Nolan's got him locked in the jailhouse in town.'

Beth knew instinctively what it was Frank wanted to discuss with her brother. 'It's about the Senorio rider who met Bronson, isn't it?'

Frank nodded, slowly, and did not open his mouth as he stared at her.

Barton sighed and waved the rangeboss to a chair. As he sat down Barton said, 'I know who helped Bronson, Frank.'

Ballinger gave a little grunt of surprise.

'My sister helped him,' stated Barton Archer. 'That's what we've been discussing.'

Ballinger turned his hat by its broad brim and watched the hat turn as he said, 'Nolan knows it was someone from here who was ridin' a black horse. When he told me that I knew exactly who it was. I didn't tell him a damned thing. I don't figure to tell him anything either. Nor will any of the men. They didn't see her ride out but they were around the yard when she came back.' Frank stopped turning the hat and gazed at Barton. 'The best this'll do is maybe buy a little time. A day or two. Nolan's going to figure it out the same way he's already figured out the rider who helped Bronson was ridin' a black horse.'

Frank sat there gazing at Barton, ignoring Beth, and waiting. Ever since Frank had been on Senorio, an Archer had made all the major decisions. Frank was perfectly agreeable to this, so he sat there waiting.

Barton, who normally handled even the most difficult cow-ranch dilemmas without more than normal delay and pondering, stood almost stoically gazing down the shadowy big yard, saying nothing.

It was Beth who broke the strained silence. 'I'll hire a lawyer from Albuquerque. Or from Denver or San Francisco if I have to go that far. Frank—Walter Bronson did *not* rob the Mesquite bank and shoot someone over there. He's never been to Mesquite. He's from Montana by way of Wyoming and Colorado. Until I met him on Senorio he knew nothing at all of this area.'

90

Frank looked down and began slowly turning his hat again. Gently he said, 'Beth, that's not our problem. That's up to Sheriff Nolan. Our problem is—you helped a feller the law was hunting.'

Barton agreed, finally. 'We have two choices, Beth. Tell Sheriff Nolan straight out, or you'll have to take the morning stage out of Marietta and go somewhere for a month or two. That will leave Frank and me to pray like hell you're right about Bronson, because if you *aren't* right, do you have any idea where that will leave Frank and me? In the same damned boat you're in; we'll have helped an outlaw's accomplice get away from the law.'

Beth's voice had iron in it when she said, 'Bob Nolan isn't our problem. It's the law over at Mesquite. All Bob will do is lock me up and hold both Walt and me. But unless they find the real bank-robber . . . Bart, you know how our law works.' She sank back down in her chair beside Frank, who was leaning there fiddling with his hat, listening without giving the impression that he was.

'Find someone, Bart, who can go over to Mesquite and—'

'Find what?' exclaimed Frank without looking up. 'That killin' and robbery took place last month! If it wasn't Bronson, then whoever it was isn't even in New Mexico Territory any more. Beth, you're talkin' about findin' a needle

91

in a damned haystack.' Frank stood up and dropped the hat upon the back of his head. 'I'll go stall Nolan. Lie to him if I have to. Get him off the ranch. Get him to go back to town if I can.' He looked over Beth's head at her brother. 'If you want, I'll come back later after Nolan's gone. By then you folks'll likely have made up your minds.'

After Frank departed, walking flatly back down across the yard where the cook was emerging over on his porch to beat the triangle for supper, Barton sank back into his chair gazing at his sister. 'This just plain stuns me, Beth. We grew up together. I was sure I understood you. Let me ask you one personal question. What is this man to you?'

She eased back in the chair with her head up, her eyes on Barton with shadows in their depths. 'I love him, Bart. And he loves me.'

'He told you that?'

'Yes. We spent another day together when I took his things up to him. Bart, that was the most wonderful day of my life.' She did not lower her eyes. 'Otherwise, I wouldn't have done anything like this to you for anything in the world.' She arose and went into the house.

He groped for the glass beside his chair, held it up, found nothing left in it, and leaned back to close his eyes and sit for a long time like that before also arising to go inside.

Jenny Plume had a magnificent beef roast

waiting. Neither of the Archers ate any supper that evening.

CHAPTER TEN

On the ride back to town Sheriff Nolan probably should have been in a grim mood, because although he had talked to most of the Senorio riders, all of whom had denied riding a black horse the day someone met Walter Bronson, and also denied seeing anyone else riding a black horse that day, Nolan was satisfied that at least some of those men *had* seen someone riding a black horse, and some of them knew who that rider was.

His last admonition to Frank Ballinger was to watch for someone to try and ride away. That, he thought, was the weakest link in his chain of circumstantial evidence, for while Frank had passed his word none of the men would escape, it was possible that in his heart Frank Ballinger would want whoever had abetted the outlaw Bronson to get off Senorio and out of the country.

But taken all together Bob Nolan was satisfied. He knew where Bronson's aid had come from. He knew that Senorio was involved. And he was confident that Barton Archer would make a particular point of seeing to it that whichever rider it was, would not leave the ranch.

He arrived back in Marietta long after dark, put up his horse and went along to the cafe where he had to rattle the door to get inside. The cafeman was not annoyed, although he probably had a right to be since he was preparing for bed. He fed Nolan and gave him a bowl of stew and some fresh coffee to take across the road with him, and although he longed to ask questions, refrained from doing so.

Nolan shed his hat at the desk, tossed the mail which had been shoved under the jailhouse door in his absence atop the scarred old table which served as his desk, then took the food down to the cell-room where Walt Bronson was lying out full length upon the bunk, wide awake.

Nolan did not say a word. He knelt, shoved the bowl and cup under the door, lighted the smoky old corridor lamp, and when Bronson came after the bowl and cup and said, 'I thought you'd forgot you had a prisoner,' Sheriff Nolan went over to lean on the bars.

'I been out at Senorio all day,' He said.

Bronson looked enquiringly out, then went over to sit upon the edge of the bunk. 'Have a nice visit?'

Nolan's reply was slow coming. 'Yeah. The grub's better out there than it is here in town.'

'Why don't you get married, then you won't have to ride so far for a decent meal?'

'Seems like an expensive way to get fed, Bronson . . . That friend of yours who brought out your gatherings, on a black horse. . .' Nolan watched for the reaction. Bronson's head came up, his eyes went swiftly to Nolan's face and remained there. The sheriff made a thin little smile. 'He'd have done better to ride a bay, then no one would have noticed, maybe.'

Bronson looked down and began eating. Just one of Nolan's words had made all the difference. It hadn't been a 'he' it had been a 'she'.

For a few moments nothing more was said, then Bronson looked up again. 'You know, Sheriff, I've heard you're a pretty good manhunter.'

Nolan answered briefly. 'I get my share.'

'But you're overlookin' something in this case, Sheriff. I really am not the man you want. Whether you believe it or not, I didn't rob that bank nor kill anyone. My point is—instead of concentrating so hard on me—since I'm locked in here and can't go anywhere—why don't you, just for the simple hell of it, see what can be turned up about the real killer?'

Nolan might have answered, but someone entering from the roadway up front caught his attention. He grunted and left Walt eating.

It was after eleven o'clock, so anyone coming to the jailhouse at this late hour would not be arriving just to pass the time.

95

The moment Nolan stepped out of the cell-room and shoved the door closed at his back, he could tell by the drawn faces of the pair of men seating themselves that what they had to tell him was not going to be encouraging.

His straw-haired slightly hawkish-looking deputy shoved out thick legs and leaned with his shoulders against the wall. The other deputy, darker and less oaken, gazed at Sheriff Nolan from a tired face. They both needed a shave and a bath. Nolan went to the table to sit down and the darker of the deputies said, 'The dog did a good job, Bob. He liked to have led us all over the damned hills, back through the mountains. I didn't know a dog could pick up a trail that old, but he sure did.'

Nolan sat waiting for the rest of it. He did not have to wait long. The hawkish man looked steadily over at Nolan wearing a tired and disgusted expression. 'Bob, if that son of a bitch raided Mesquite, he did it from the air. His sign went dang near due north right on up through the damned mountains from where he finally came down and hit the stageroad. And from there he went west. . . He didn't come from the east at all. . . Unless that damned hound-dog was in cahoots with him an' led us on a different trail, which no dog's smart enough to do.'

The smaller deputy added a little more. 'We found three camps. Sheriff, that feller came from the *north*, and in case you're figuring that

96

he went north out of Mesquite then cut around westerly so's he'd be coming down-country into our area,' the deputy adamantly shook his head. 'He didn't do any such a thing.'

Nolan said, 'You're sure?'

'As sure as I am that I'm settin' here right this minute,' replied the deputy. 'We met the stager from Mesquite over the rim and part way down across Ripgut Meadow toward Summersville. He was in Mesquite the day before. They got word from some rangemen that the outlaw went straight south in the direction of the Mex border. The stager told us the law over there's got a posse down south scouring after that feller, and they also got word to the Border Patrol that he's headin' their way.'

Bob Nolan eased back in his chair. After a moment of sober reflection he said, 'Gawddammit.'

The fair-haired deputy scowled. 'Yeah. We worked our butts off and worked that hound dog until his pads was tender—for nothing.'

Nolan's eyes flashed. 'How the hell was I to know?'

The deputy did not back off. 'Maybe you wasn't, Bob, but that don't change anything. I'm going to take two, three days off.' He arose, thick and massive, and unpleasant. 'Seems to me you should have kept more in touch with the law over at Mesquite.' He went to the door, paused with one ham-sized paw on the latch, then went stalking out into the late night.

The other deputy also arose, but he was less intractable than his partner. He said, 'Too bad it had to turn out this way, Bob. You got the wrong man in the cells. Maybe it wouldn't be a bad idea if you was to contact the law over at Mesquite.' Then he also departed leaving Sheriff Nolan sitting there in acute discomfort.

He had been so positive.

Later, he normally would have retrieved the bowl and cup from the cell, but tonight he did not want to have to look at Bronson, so he simply doused the lights, locked up for the night and headed for his room at the boarding-house.

In the morning he felt no better, but he was at least resigned, so he wrote a letter to the authorities over at Mesquite requesting information on the status of their investigation, and delivered it by hand to the driver who was preparing to take the early-morning stage out of Marietta on the eastward run.

Then he went glumly to the cafe, ate a big breakfast, got another platter of steak and spuds and sourdough dumplings and took it across to his cell-room.

Bronson was waiting. When he saw the food he cocked a baffled eye at Sheriff Nolan. 'That's the kind of meal they give a condemned man before the hanging,' he said, and leaned to pick up the platter.

Nolan cleared his throat. 'You tell me who

helped you, Bronson, and I'll make a trade with you.'

Walt took the platter to the bunk and put it over there before straightening around shaking his head. 'No thanks.'

Nolan shifted position in the corridor, leaned upon the cell-front and unhappily regarded his prisoner. 'All right. I'll tell you the rest of it. I'll turn you loose.'

Walt stared, then sauntered over closer and continued to stare. Finally, as a suspicion formed, he smiled without any warmth and said, 'If I tell you who helped me you'll turn me loose? Sheriff, you've discovered that I'm not the man you're looking for, haven't you?'

Nolan had been seeking a face-saving way out of this. Now, he could clear his conscience, but at the expense of his reputation as an unerring manhunter by answering truthfully. Fortunately, he had more conscience than conceit, so he nodded his head. 'I think so. It'll be a few days before I'm plumb certain. But I'll take the chance and turn you loose—after you tell me who your accomplice was.'

Walt was smiling again, without warmth, when he answered, 'You can go to hell, Sheriff.'

He turned, went over to eat his breakfast and did it with his back to the corridor. When eventually he turned Sheriff Nolan was no longer in sight.

In fact Sheriff Nolan was up in the front office

99

coaxing a fire under the coffeepot, irritated by the way Bronson had come out ahead, and also by the way Bronson had reacted a few minutes earlier, although, and Nolan was fair enough to admit this, if their positions had been reversed, Bob Nolan would have been a lot more violently hostile.

There was a big freight wagon entering town from the south, its owner evidently anxious to off-load over at the loading-dock out behind the general store before the heat arrived.

Nolan heard a dog excitedly barking, then a man's bawling profanity as the freighter or his swamper cursed the dog. Nolan went to the jailhouse door from force of habit and looked out. The freighter had four span of mules on the tongue and several looked to be young, green animals; they were beginning to show fear, near panic, as the dog worried them. Nolan saw the freighter reach down for his Winchester and left the doorway heading straight for the barking dog. He ignored the freighter, came in behind the dog, and because the dog was concentrating on trying to nip a mule's heels he had no idea anyone was back there until Sheriff Nolan's hands closed down, one across the dog's back, the other one at the back of his head so that he would be unable to turn and bite. Then Sheriff Nolan turned and hurled the dog through the air. It struck the jailhouse front wall, fell in a howling heap, unscrambled itself and fled at top speed.

The big freighter shoved his carbine back under his legs and said, 'You should have busted his damned back.'

Nolan pointed. 'That's the road leads down into the alley behind the store,' and walked on over to the general store to purchase two sacks of Bull Durham, and the wheat-straw cigarette papers that went with the tobacco. The storekeeper had seen the interlude in the roadway and thanked Nolan. He then said, 'That's my daughter's dog. I'm glad you didn't let the freighter shoot it.'

Nolan's frame of mind was not very compassionate. 'Your daughter had ought to bust a fence slat over that dog's butt every time he goes after something like that.'

The storekeeper agreed. He had seen anger in Sheriff Nolan before. 'I'll make sure she does it, Sheriff. By the way, that freighter's bringin' in some malt whiskey from El Paso. I'll sure set a bottle aside for you, if you want me to.'

'How much?'

The storekeeper spread his hands. 'Nothing. For keepin' the freighter from shooting the dog.'

Nolan returned to the road feeling slightly mollified, and set to work rolling his first smoke of the day. He was right partial to malt whiskey. The variety they served across the bar at the saloon northward up the roadway was rye whiskey, as pale and green as pure rotgut.

Frank Ballinger was coming down the roadway in a flat-footed walk, the horse under him moving along with the gait of an animal accustomed to covering long distance in open country.

Nolan looked up with surprise. Frank rarely visited town, and almost never during daytime. He lit the cigarette and watched as Frank turned in at the hitch-rack across in front of the jailhouse and swung down.

Nolan walked over there to meet Frank's level, unsmiling look. Nolan said, 'Nice morning, Frank... That feller didn't get spooked and run for it did he?'

Frank pushed past and entered the jailhouse office without opening his mouth. He shoved back his hat, tugged off his roping gloves and fished inside his shirt for an envelope which he tossed upon the table. Then he spoke.

'Bart sent this note to you. He'd have come himself except that ... he sent me instead.'

Nolan looked from the envelope to the *segundo*. A premonition kept him from reaching for the envelope. 'It's about that feller who helped Bronson?'

Frank said, 'All you got to do, Bob, is open it and find out for yourself... Yeah; that's what it's about.'

Nolan sat down, tore open the envelope, extracted the folded paper with one curt paragraph on it, read, then re-read, and finally let the paper slip from his fingers to the desk-top.

Frank turned his back, stepped to the stove, hefted the coffeepot and drew himself off a cup. Then he turned, pale eyes showing hard irony. 'You're the law,' he said, and made a mock salute with the cup before drinking from it.

Sheriff Nolan glanced down at the note again. 'Beth...?'

Frank said nothing. He drained the cup and set it aside, then pulled forth his gloves and began to methodically put them on. When he was finished he gave Nolan a hard look. 'Yeah, Beth. What are you going to do about it?'

Sheriff Nolan leaned back. 'I'll be double damned,' he muttered. 'It never even occurred to me it could have been her.'

'Well, it should have,' growled Frank. 'Where'n hell did you think that blue napkin came from? You never been in a bunkhouse in your life where they use stuff like that.'

Nolan glanced upwards at the hard-faced, tough older man. He had been so occupied with other aspects of his manhunt he had quite forgotten the damned blue cloth napkin. 'Sit down,' he said. Frank continued to stand in front of the stove, lanky, weathered and clearly hostile. Nolan pointed to a bench. 'Sit down! I got something to tell you that you can take back to Mister Archer for me.'

Frank sat, but only upon the edge of the bench and he was clearly not going to stay there for long.

Nolan shifted some scattered papers atop his table, and while looking down as he did this he said, 'I'm going to turn Bronson loose.'

Frank stared, sitting as motionless as stone.

'They're chasin' the feller who raided Mesquite down south. Seems he's heading for the Mex line.' Nolan finally raised his face. For a moment the two men stared at one another, then Nolan spoke again. 'If the damned fool hadn't run that night I was out there...'

Frank surprised Nolan by saying, 'Yeah. That's what I thought. If he'd stayed in the yard...' Frank arose slowly. 'How long you know Bronson wasn't the feller?'

'Since last night. Want another cup of coffee?'

'No. But for jailhouse coffee it's not too bad.'

Nolan could not tell from looking at the *segundo* how genuinely pleased Frank was, but he could tell from the rough civility which Frank was showing. 'I'll turn him out maybe tomorrow or the day after. I got to get official verification from Mesquite. It might come back on the night stage, but I figure it'll more likely arrive tomorrow or the next day.' Nolan went to the tie-rack out front with old Frank, and as the rangeboss was gathering his reins Nolan said. 'Beth ... I never in this lifetime would have thought of her as doin' that.'

Frank swung up. 'Sure you would have, Bob. In time. That's what we figured an' that's why Bart sent you that note... But you wouldn't have been able to ride out and haul her back to your jailhouse.' Frank smiled broadly. 'She's not at the ranch.' He reined back and turned to go trotting up out of town.

CHAPTER ELEVEN

Nolan's reaction to Frank Ballinger's last remark before the *segundo* left town came slowly. He had been too surprised to learn the identity of the individual who had aided Bronson.

But eventually he reacted. If Beth Archer was not at Senorio it meant that her brother, and probably old Frank too, had decided to put her beyond reach of the law, which of course made them conspirators. That annoyed Bob Nolan; but it was nothing he could do anything about in the light of developments since last night, when his deputies had returned.

She hadn't really abetted a criminal even though she and everyone else had certainly thought that she had—except Bronson.

Nolan went back down to the cells and Walt Bronson met him as he usually had, with an expression of calm confidence. 'You got the

105

key?' he asked. Nolan shook his head. 'Not quite yet. When it's verified the authorities over at Mesquite know who the raider is.' Nolan leaned on the bars. 'I know who your friend was on the black horse.'

Walt was gazing directly at Sheriff Nolan. The lawman's expression said enough so Walt's retort was curt. 'One person had faith in me, Nolan.'

The sheriff shrugged. 'I'm not sure a woman's faith in a man—under some circumstances—is based on faith.'

'Intuition then.'

Nolan sighed. 'That's plumb silly. Anyway, her brother sent Frank in with a note a while back admitting it was Beth who helped you . . . Bronson, I'll say one thing for you—you got good taste in women. I've known Beth Archer for years and never once saw her even look a second time at a man. I sort of figured she was gettin' like old Frank—didn't think about anything but Senorio.'

Someone came noisily into the office up front and yelled for Sheriff Nolan. He turned and hastened up out of the cell-room. There had been an urgency in that shout.

The excited man was grey and lined and agitated. His name was Martin Stevens. He was the Marietta superintendent for the New Mexico Stage and Cartage Company, and right at this moment he was indignant, worried, and very agitated. He did not wait until Nolan had closed the cell-room door before loudly saying, 'My south coach's been stopped. Some son of a bitch has taken off two of the horses and left a rode-down saddle animal, and left like he'd been shot out of a cannon.'

'Robbed the coach?' asked Nolan.

'No. Well, he took a Winchester off the driver, but this was a freight run—no passengers, just some boxes of light minin' machinery for those fellers in the north mountains got that chrome mine up there. No, he didn't do anythin' but stop the coach, take off two horses, the Winchester, and run west like the devil was ahind him. Sheriff, those horses are worth a hundred dollars each. The company'll raise hell and prop it up.'

'Rode west?' said Nolan. 'Did your driver get a good look at him?'

'Yeah. Tall, skinny feller with brown hair down over his collar, with an ivory handle on his sixgun and walked with a noticeable limp. Young, the driver said, and hadn't shaved in a couple weeks or more. Bad, the driver said; mean-lookin' and bad.'

Nolan considered the element of time. 'How long ago did he stop the coach, Martin?'

The stage company superintendent paused and frowned. Then he answered. 'About three hours back. The driver, what with a load and all, had to walk his remainin' two horses the full

107

distance to town. It's taken him about three hours. The feller stopped the coach down south about where the road forks to the east.'

'Three hours head-start,' said Nolan, more to himself than to the other man. '*Two* horses; why in hell would a man take *two* horses to replace a rode-down one?'

The older man agitatedly said, 'I got no idea, but I know the longer we stand aroun' here talkin' the farther that son of a bitch is gettin' with company livestock. Sheriff—if you got up a posse and—'

'Yeah,' Nolan cut in dryly, 'and wasted another hour doing that . . . All right, Martin, go on back to the corralyard. When I get back I'll come look you up.'

As the agitated older man moved toward the door he looked back. 'The company'll pay you for bringin' our livestock back.'

Nolan scarcely heard. There had not been a stage robbery in the Marietta countryside in many years, and as he went to the wall-rack for a booted Winchester he reflected that this hadn't actually been a robbery—well—horse-stealing was robbery, but when stage-coaches were stopped the harness animals were left intact, it was the passengers, the mail pouches, and the bullion if there was any, that ordinarily were a highwayman's target.

Nolan suddenly remembered something. Last night one of his deputies had said he was going to take two or three days off, and the other one, without saying that, had certainly acted as though he too might do it. Nolan left the saddleboot by the door and went legging it up to the boarding-house. He found, not the darker deputy, but the hawk-faced, burly one. He was sitting on the porch up there looking sour as the sheriff came along.

Nolan said, 'Where's Evan?' and the straw-haired deputy shrugged while answering. 'I don't know. Except that he rode out real early this mornin' with his fishing pole.' The burly, bull-necked man glanced up. 'Why?'

'Some son of a bitch stopped the south stage a few hours back and took off two of the horses, then rode west.'

The deputy's brows dropped a notch. 'Two harness horses . . . that's all?'

'Yeah. And left a worn-out saddle horse behind. Martin's having fits.'

'Couple hours ago?'

'More like three accordin' to Martin.' For a moment longer Bob Nolan stood there, then turned to hasten down to Rudell's liverybarn. Behind him the burly deputy struggled up out of his chair and turned toward the door at his back. 'I'll get my guns. Tell Rudell to saddle me a fresh horse. Not my horse, he got his butt rode off lately. A fresh, strong one.'

Nolan turned, but his deputy was already hastening toward his room for his spurs, hat

109

and guns.

By the time Sheriff Nolan got down abreast of the jailhouse a dusty, gauntleted man with a big red neckerchief was reaching to open the door, and turned as Nolan said, 'Can't do much for you right now, *amigo*. I got a horsethief to hunt down.'

Nolan reached past for the booted Winchester as the other man drew back, then fished out an envelope and wordlessly handed it over. As Nolan accepted it the man said, 'I drive stage for Martin Stevens on the Mesquite run. A deputy over there give me this letter for the sheriff over here just as I was pullin' out last night. I figured it was urgent so I brought it right over.'

Nolan looked at the crumpled envelope, then said, 'Thanks.'

The stager nodded and turned away.

Nolan ripped open the envelope, read the letter, then swore under his breath and entered the jailhouse moving rapidly. He went down to the cell-room, opened Bronson's door and made a curt gesture. 'You're on your own. Your horse is down at the liverybarn. I'm in a hell of a hurry right now. Later, when I get back, I'll look you up and we'll talk.'

Nolan left Walt standing in the cell doorway and hurried back up through, grabbed up his saddle-boot again and left the jailhouse walking briskly southward.

Down at Webster Rudell's liverybarn he

called out before he was even in the doorway. A startled dayman blinked, then, sensing the urgency, ran to comply. The liveryman, a frail, small, bow-legged man with pale grey eyes and a perpetual squint, poked his head from the harness-room, then shoved on out into the runway.

'What the hell's goin' on?' he asked.

Nolan asked for a strong, durable horse for Deputy Jack Parton, and sketchily explained about the horse theft. Rudell reacted swiftly, and with the best of reasons; if there was one person aside from working stockmen who loathed horsethieves, it was liverymen.

Normally, Rudell did not rig horses out; he had a dayman for that, but this time he went to work with swift, sure hands. By the time the hawk-faced deputy got down there, and knelt to buckle his spurs into place, Rudell and his dayman were half-finished.

The deputy straightened up, re-adjusted his sagging gunbelt and said, 'He went west?'

Nolan's answer was offered as he strode toward the horse Rudell's dayman had finished with. 'West, riding one and I guess leading the other one . . . Jack?'

The deputy walked over to buckle his booted saddlegun under the *rosadero*. 'What?'

'Thanks.'

The deputy grunted, finished with the boot and took the reins from Webster Rudell to

111

dourly lead the big sorrel gelding out front before mounting.

As they rode out of town the hawk-faced deputy scanned the open countryside and for a long while kept pace with Nolan in sombre silence. Eventually, as they were angling southward but on a westerly course because Nolan wanted to pick up the tracks out where the outlaw was heading, not back where he had been, Parton said, 'He didn't rob the passengers?'

Nolan explained that the stage had not been carrying passengers, only light freight, but Parton was not satisfied with that.

'There was a driver, wasn't there?'

Nolan looked around. 'Jack, this son of a bitch was running. I don't know what he was running from, but he'd ridden his horse down and wanted to keep running. My guess is that the only thing he saw with horseflesh attached to it was Martin's stagecoach.'

The deputy looked back, then southward, and shook his head. 'I don't see anyone.'

Nolan hadn't seen any pursuers either and he had been looking for them since they'd left the lower end of town, but that did not have to mean anything; if someone was hot in pursuit, they might not have got over this far yet, or, for that matter, they might not even be directly behind the fugitive. What Nolan was especially concerned with was the horsethief; whatever

112

else was involved, he would find out in time, but for the moment his immediate concern was the man he was angling westerly to locate, by the man's fresh tracks. And he found them, eventually miles below Marietta and several miles west.

There was no question about the authenticity of the tracks. For one thing there were two harness-horses. For another thing the imprints were much larger than the shod-horse marks a saddlehorse would leave.

Deputy Parton's dourness vanished as soon as he and Sheriff Nolan swung due west over those harness-horse tracks. He smiled for the first time that day, studied the onward flow of countryside, and made a shrewd guess.

'He dassn't stay out here for long, Sheriff. There's rangeriders all over the country this time of year. They're bound to wonder about someone ridin' one harness-horse and leadin' another one.'

'A fleeing man runs in a straight line—if he's scairt enough, Jack.'

Parton concentrated on the tracks for several miles, then straightened in the saddle when Nolan pointed out a banner of dust dead ahead in the distance. Parton said, 'Senorio's crew.' He gave no reason why he thought those were Senorio's men up yonder, but he and the sheriff had been riding on Senorio range for more than an hour, so it was a good guess.

Nolan slackened gait, hauled all the way down to a walk, and where the harness-horse tracks suddenly veered northward, Nolan said, 'I don't think he's too far ahead, Jack. I think he probably saw that dust too, and decided to head up-country.' Nolan squinted at the area where men working cattle were raising all that dust. 'If he *did* turn off because of the dust, then it wasn't too long ago before he passed this way.'

They turned northward. By now they were six or seven miles west of Marietta with a high sun burning downward. An accumulation of mild heat-haze was settling. It somewhat obscured the details of the land but not any of the prominent characteristics.

Nolan had no canteen. Neither did his deputy have one, but they had not been concerned with something like that. Nor, in a country as well watered as this seemingly endless run of range country, was there a need for either men or animals to go dry for very long.

At the southern extremity of Archer Creek where the horsethief had paused in thin willow-shade to water his horses, Nolan and Parton did the same. Then they splashed on across and Nolan pointed: the tracks showed darkly for a hundred yards onward, which meant that, as hot as it now was, unless those wet tracks had been quite fresh, the water would have evaporated.

Parton was encouraged. 'We're gaining.'

114

Then he straightened in the saddle to squint ahead. 'And that son of a bitch'll see us coming, once he gets into the hills where he's got a little height to look down from.'

There was nothing to be done about that, obviously. Nolan considered the distance they still had to cover before they were also into the hills. His interest now had less to do with being seen than it had to do with being ambushed because they had been seen.

The heat was punishing. The closer they got to the hills the more it seemed to bounce back from the slopes and roll back down in shimmery waves out across the range. In the far northeast, partially hidden by a thrust of high mountains, there was an irregular rank of clouds and the sky over there had a brassiness, a kind of hard sheen to it.

The only shade for a couple of miles was along the uneven course of Archer Creek, and since this was the logical route for anyone to travel, not only because of the welcome shade but also because the willows over there and the flourishing, green thickets, provided a protective shield, that became the route the lawmen followed, still riding along the trail of the fleeing man.

CHAPTER TWELVE

The heat which had increased gradually through a clear, perfect morning, was less noticeable in Marietta because the buildings provided shade until about noon. Then, with an orange sun hanging directly overhead the only relief was inside buildings.

It was not uncommon for summer to arrive abruptly in New Mexico. Most people were accustomed to it, were inured to the heat, which was with them for most of the year.

It was rangemen who developed a tolerance for the heat. They were out in it every day, but to someone like Walt Bronson who had come from an area where winter, spring and autumn were usually cold, and where the people built up more of an immunity to cold than to heat, the ride out of Marietta shortly before mid-day was like leaving an oasis and heading into a desert.

He felt the force of heat, of course, but being free again alleviated the initial discomfort, and an hour later sweat under his shirt helped somewhat. Nor did he set a course which would keep him riding unprotected beneath that smoky sun.

He drifted toward the far-away hills whose scattered stands of timber offered shade, and he was not in a particular hurry. He had his bedroll and saddlebags along; except for one thing there was not even much reason for him to remain in the country, but as he angled toward the Saginaw hills with their darker, high and more massively impressive mountains farther back, he did not even consider riding on.

Once, he saw three riders hazing a band of horses in a southwesterly direction and assumed those would be Senorio horses and riders, although the distance was far too great to make any kind of positive identification, and by the time he was in the hills the land below was empty, the heat was solid, and off to the northwest barely showing over high rims, a rank of uneven clouds seemed to be hovering, seemed to be waiting perhaps until nightfall before they began their march down over the countryside.

He headed up the upper reaches of Archer Creek, got over there and found the place where someone had once made a camp, re-arranged the stones where ancient coals showed darkly, and set his horse to graze, hobbled, while he took his time about setting up a camp in thick oak-shade.

He settled comfortably atop his unfurled bedroll, tipped down his hat, and napped. There was an occasional soft breeze at this elevation, and that helped. There was also the feeling of peace in the empty solitude of the hills. A number of things which he had missed during his stay at the Marietta jailhouse, such as the lack of anxiety, made him sleep well and without disturbance, until his horse nickered, then he awakened, listened for a recurrence and when there was none, he rolled onto his back looking up through dark oak leaves at the position of the sun. He had slept about two and a half hours, the afternoon was waning, his stomach was making complaining sounds, and he sat up, stretched, looked all around, then arose to go delve in his saddlebags for the flat sardine tins he, like many rangemen, usually carried along as emergency rations.

Later, with the sun sinking, he found a pool in the creek, stripped, bathed, and sat among some willows battling mosquitoes until he was dry, then hastily re-dressed.

The heat did not diminish when the sun sank. In fact, for an hour or two it seemed to increase. Walt went out to make certain the hobbled horse had plenty of grass, remained out there for a while, then returned to camp and bedded down.

As far as he knew, no one knew where he was, and no one else was in the hills anywhere around. He liked that idea; as with most rangemen who had lived solitary lives a good bit of the time, Walt Bronson did not object to being solitary at all. In fact he liked it. Not all the time, but occasionally, when the mood was on him to be alone, as it now was.

He awakened ahead of dawn, looked out where his horse was still sleeping, standing with one hind leg cocked, with his head down and the lower lip sagging. Walt smiled, arose, took his old towel and chunk of lye-soap to head back for the creek.

While he was washing the call of a distant horse floated down to him. Perhaps some Senorio horses had got into the hills. If so, Senorio riders would find them and chase them back down out of there. Walt had heard Frank mention keeping the loose-stock out on the range, away from wolf and cougar country.

He finished washing and returned to camp, finished more sardines, then made a smoke and sat in the pleasant sunshine with his back against the tipped-up saddle, looking back down in the direction of Marietta, and later, out over Senorio range in the direction of the home-ranch.

He probably should have headed back there yesterday. He probably should have ridden into the yard, hunted up Beth, and talked with her. He did not owe another human being on this earth anything, but he owed her. Not just for helping him, but for having faith in him.

He killed the smoke thinking of their last day together. *That* was what kept him where he was, in the lower rolling country of the Saginaw hills.

He struck camp when the morning was mid-way along, rode westerly through the hills before the heat arrived, and topped out along a timbered sidehill where by looking southward he could see folds of hills, vastly more forested over this far, which seemed to form a rough drainage system toward a horseshoe-shaped tall-grass meadow.

He knew where he was even though he could not see the blue-water pond. She had called it the Piney Woods. He angled back and forth picking his way down in that direction. The heat was noticeable even up through the forested slopes, which meant it was much hotter out where there was no protection.

His horse, after its long rest in town, sweated more than it normally did, but it had not been confined so long that it tired easily. The descent, in some ways, was harder for the horse than climbing into the mountains had been, but when it finally got down where the timber was not so thick and the way required less forethought at picking a passage, the horse loosened, lengthened his stride and appeared to take more interest. Probably because the fragrance of unedible pine needles was being superseded by the mouth-watering scent of grass.

Where they came out into the pond-area at its northernmost perimeter the heat was mitigated, no doubt because of the expanse of clear water, but the sun had its way out there too; it reflected off the pond with painful brilliance.

Walt let the horse head out and around to the grass on the west side, which was where he had hobbled her horse and his horse, once. Where he stopped, finally, he had the smooth old veiny rock in plain sight at the water's edge. Without really considering why, he dismounted, off-saddled, hobbled his animal and walked over to the big rock. There, he grinned in recollection; he must have looked ridiculous wading out there as gingerly as a timid child.

He had bathed the day before so he felt no urge to repeat that, particularly here where the water was deep, but he sat down, kicked out of his boots, hauled up his trouser-legs, and smiling to himself, waded out into the shallows again. This time, he was bolder, but when the mud underfoot began sloping outward, he avoided it. He was not ready to be *that* bold.

His horse stopped cropping grass, threw up its head and intently stared toward some distant trees where speckled shade lay in a motley overlie which made it almost impossible to separate one silhouette from another. But the horse was not concerned with an identity, he was concerned with a scent.

He did not move a muscle as he stared, for a long while there was no movement, then a horse swished its tail. Moments later a rangy, lanky man lifted his rein-hand to turn the horse back up through the trees, and for a second or two sunshine highlighted an unsmiling, bronzed-weathered craggy countenance, then the rider had his back to the pond as he threaded his way westward up through the trees.

Those gathering clouds off in the north-east were finally beginning to move. But very slowly, perhaps because there was as little wind aloft as there was down below.

Bronson walked up out of the water into the grass, and met a sleek, big fat gopher-snake. They were mutually surprised. The snake lifted its head to look upwards and Bronson felt as though his naked feet had suddenly became enormous; that if the snake came closer he was going to bump into ten bare toes, and although Walt knew how harmless the big snake was, it was nonetheless an unsettling confrontation. Then the snake, reassured by the utter stillness of the man, glided away; kept looking back and seemed to be restraining an urge to flee in panic, and glided out through the tall grass in the direction of the pond. He could swim; most snakes could swim, but they had to want to do it badly because they were more vulnerable to eagles or hawks, or even large fish when afloat than they were in the mud and grass of the shallows.

Walt sat on Beth's big boulder to dry his feet and legs. Once, he turned to look at the bay horse. It was grazing again, a picture of equine contentment. Bronson leaned, tipped down his hatbrim and wiggled his toes in the bright sunlight.

He felt restless. If Nolan knew Beth had

abetted him, then surely her brother also knew because that information could only have come from Senorio. That also meant Frank must know too, which probably meant that Walt Bronson would not be welcome back at the home-ranch. Nor did he hold it against Barton Archer that he would disapprove of his sister becoming involved with a drifter, a man who owned a fine big breedy bay horse and very little else.

Still, Walt intended to see Beth. His sojourn in the Marietta jailhouse had mellowed the ardour which had gripped him since he and Beth had spent that last day together, but it had not lessened his strong feelings toward her. He would see her again and this time they would be more practical. At least that is what he thought as he sat there waiting for his feet to dry. They would talk as reasonable people. He had absolutely nothing to offer her, except his love, and while that was a lot—at least he felt that it was a lot—one hundred and fifty thousand acres, thousands of head of cattle, wealth, comfort and absolute security, made an overwhelming balance in the other side of the scale.

He sat up, shoved back his hat, swore under his breath and reached for his socks and boots. Loving someone, he was discovering, might be the most exhilarating, intense emotion a human being could experience, but it was also compounded of more intense anxiety, fear, something bordering upon desperation, and total insecurity, than people would ordinarily experience who were *not* in love.

He rolled and lit a smoke, gazed moodily southward down the length of the horseshoe-meadow in the direction of the open range, neglected to notice that the sun was moving a little off centre, or that those massive clouds were closing their ranks as they moved with ponderous slowness over the highest top-outs on what appeared to be an east-to-southwest course, and also neglected to look over where his horse was switching its tail at flies because in the distance someone was angling directly toward the broad mouth of the Piney Woods cove, aiming unerringly for the area where Bronson was sitting.

The speck grew larger by the moment. It was a rider, there was no question of that. Bronson felt nothing until the speck assumed recognisable although distant dimensions, then his heart beat with a more solid, steady cadence. He *hoped* with all his might that it would be her, but there was no reason he could imagine why it would be. As far as he knew, she still thought he was in the Marietta jailhouse.

Sunshine without its earlier orange flame, softened the world and brought forth more colour. It was a black horse!

Slowly Bronson got to his feet, re-set his hat

124

then stood like a stone with the hope steadily rising. It *was* her! When she came up through the horseshoe-meadow he could make out a white sleeveless blouse; no rangeman in his right mind ever wore anything like that. She was hatless, and that too was something a rangeman would avoid. Then he could see the horse better, recognised it as the one she had been riding the day she had brought him the bedroll and saddlebags, and finally, when she pulled down to a trot, he saw the fullness of the white blouse, the ease and assurance of her posture in the saddle, and began to slowly smile.

How she had happened to come up here did not for the moment concern him, except that he knew this was one of her favourite places. All that mattered was that it was Beth, and she had seen him, had surely recognised him, and was coming to him.

CHAPTER THIRTEEN

She stood beside her horse, flushed and a little breathless, then she dropped the reins and ran into his arms as though she were a girl, not a woman. Her grip was powerful, surprisingly so. When her head came up the eyes were darker than they had ever been. Walt kissed her. She responded with an almost fiercely possessive fire which momentarily upset him, then she pushed clear and said, 'It *was* you.' And before that made sense to him, she explained. 'Frank was up here. He saw a bay horse he thought looked like your animal, and he saw a man wading in the pond. He—we met—on the range about three miles from here. He told me . . . Then he told me something else . . .'

'That Sheriff Nolan turned me loose?'

'No. We knew that would happen. Not this soon. We thought it would be tomorrow or the next day . . . Frank told me—to come up here and see if it was you.'

Walt gazed at her. For Frank Ballinger to say something like that was completely out of character. Frank had never said a word to Bronson unless it was about work. Bronson had never seen Frank smile nor show any softness.

She watched his expression, interpreted it correctly, and, taking his hand to go over by the boulder where they could sit, she said, 'I know how the men think of Frank. But with me—he's always been different. More so after my father died.' She pulled him down at her side, squeezed his hand then released it.

'He knew it was you. He didn't say that, but he knew . . . He also knew the rest of it. Maybe Bart told him, maybe he guessed it.' With scarcely any interval, she jumped to another topic. 'My brother decided to tell Sheriff Nolan I was the person who helped you. Frank and I were with him when he made his mind up about that. Bart said Bob Nolan would figure it out shortly anyway. Then he and Frank sent me to a line-cabin we have in the mountains. I was to stay there until it was safe to return . . . I believe Bart shared my conviction that you weren't a robber and a murderer, but all he told me was that he'd hire detectives and lawyers.' She leaned back against the rock, gazing at his profile. 'Walt, I stayed in the darned cabin until I couldn't stand it one more minute, then I came back down . . . Frank was upset about that when we met this morning—when he told me you were up here. He said I was endangering them all. But he also said, if I wanted to see you, it was all right with him; he'd manage to keep Bart and the riders away from the Piney Woods. He told me to take you back up to that line-cabin in the mountains and hide you.'

'Hide me?'

'You escaped didn't you?'

He stared at her for a moment, but of course she nor Frank nor her brother had been in town this morning when Sheriff Nolan had turned him out. 'No, I didn't escape. Nolan let me go yesterday right after breakfast.'

'He found out that soon you weren't the renegade?'

'All I can tell you is that he unlocked the door, said we'd talk later, and left in a big hurry. You don't have to hide me and Frank doesn't have to be afraid I'm a fugitive.'

She put both hands behind her head and leaned, looking out where her black gelding had ambled over to pick grass with his bay horse. 'The entire thing is Bob Nolan's fault,' she said. 'He came out here—jumped to a conclusion because you fitted a description he had, and now look at the mess he's made.'

Walt wasn't looking at anything but her, nor did he have much success thinking about anything but her. 'Forget Nolan,' he told her. 'There is something else . . .'

She turned, seemed to sense his dilemma, and brought her hands down as she faced him. 'You have a wife somewhere.'

He shook his head. 'I told you I wasn't married. No—but it's probably as bad. I don't have anything. See that bay horse yonder and the saddle in the grass?'

She kept staring at him. 'You're not going to tell me how much I'll be giving up, are you?'

He reddened; he'd never talked this personally with a woman before, nor did it sit well with him that she had anticipated him. 'That's exactly what I'm telling you.'

She leaned. 'Walt, what do you think I've been turning over and over in my mind since you let me ride away that last time we were together?' She did not let him reply. 'A woman always gives up a lot. She has to; she can't live at home and have all that security, and still be in love with a man—and want him—want to be with him all the time.' She raised a hand to his face, then took it away. 'I can tell you a little about being in love, Walt. It's pain—and a whole lot more—but the pain is there and it's real.'

He had made this identical discovery. 'That's true, Beth. But what I've been thinking is—if you went with me there'd probably be a lot of disillusionment as well, and hardship, and—'

'Walt, I've waited a lot longer than most women wait to fall in love. I'm not a dewy-eyed girl. I know what's coming—sacrifice—and I'm not only willing, I *want* to do it. Don't ask me why. All I can tell you is that it's *there*.' She put a hand between her breasts over her heart. 'I've thought and thought. All the time you were in jail I rode out, and sat under the trees, and thought... Walt?'

'Yes.'

'Do you love me?'

'Yes. You know I do.'

'Enough...?'

He smiled. 'Yes. More than enough. But Beth you'll be giving up everything you know for a man you barely know.'

'Jenny told me the wisest man alive cannot understand a woman... I just told you—I'll give it up. I'll give it up right this instant.'

He reached and she came over to him. When he started to speak she shook her head and

129

sought his mouth with her lips. She kept him silent with a searing kiss that dissolved every practical thought in his mind.

Afterwards she clung to him, buried her face against his chest and mutedly said, 'Are you hungry? I have some food in my saddlebags.'

He had not expected her to say anything that practical but he was glad she had because he did not know where to take their conversation otherwise. 'I was hungry an hour ago but right now I couldn't even eat a piece of oven-hot apple pie.'

She drew closer. 'Come up to the line-cabin with me.'

'Now?'

'Yes.'

She pulled back, raised a hand to brush back a heavy coil of black hair, and showed a flushed face. 'Ready?'

They arose and went out to the horses, rigged up in total silence, swung up and as she took the lead she turned, and smiled.

He shook his head. One of her smiles melted every vestige of obstinacy in him. 'You're—'

'Yes, I know. A vixen. I've been thinking about that too. Give me a little time. I don't have any experience, but I think this comes naturally to a woman.'

He elected not to pursue this topic. Not right at this moment as they worked their way up out of the horseshoe meadow, through the trees and into the cooler elevations. Later, he would, he told himself. Later, he would tell her all the things *he'd* thought about in the jail cell. He had a hunch they would not be very different from the things she had thought about.

Down through the spindly pines at the lower west side of the horseshoe meadow a solitary, craggy-faced rider had watched their progress up into the forested foothills. Now, he turned and rode southward back down to the open country, then booted his horse over into a long lope aiming directly for Senorio's home-place. Old Frank Ballinger did not believe Beth was doing the right thing, but instinct told him no one in this world could convince her otherwise. And maybe *he* was wrong. He was honest enough with himself to acknowledge that he did not know a damned thing about this sort of affair.

He had liked Walter Bronson—the short length of time he had known him—but for almost twenty years he'd been a sort of surrogate father to Beth Archer, and Barton too but less so with Barton; it troubled him that she had fallen in love. By the time he was two-thirds of the way back to the home-place he had come to the conclusion that by himself he would be unable to sort through his powerful protective instincts, and his inherent, natural dourness, let alone his almost total ignorance of personal love between a man and a woman, so he would seek Bart out.

131

Maybe Bart wouldn't be any better, but at least between the two of them they would be able to come up with something.

When he reached the yard with dusk on the way and saw Sheriff Nolan on the veranda of the main-house with Bart, he felt like swearing. That damned sheriff had lately become a burr under Frank's saddleblanket. Of all the times for him to show up, why did he have to do it this afternoon!

Frank put up his horse, taking his time in the hope that Nolan would leave. He looked out. Nolan was still over there. Frank swore and went out back to fork feed to the corralled horses. Then he walked to the rack out behind the bunkhouse and washed, combed his hair and rolled a smoke. Some of the riders were drifting in. He heard them entering the yard, and heard them talking out front of the barn where they dismounted. He stepped around the edge of the bunkhouse and looked.

Nolan and his horse were gone.

Without further delay Frank trudged across the yard, and as Barton moved toward the door to enter the house, Frank sang out to him. Barton turned, then stepped away from the door waiting.

Frank was one of those individuals who made no attempt to conceal his sentiments. His face was an open book, and after one glance Barton mdoved back to the centre of the porch as he

132

said, 'Trouble?'

Frank told him bluntly about meeting Beth, about knowing who that had been at the Piney Woods pond. He said he'd told Beth Bronson was up there, and because he saw the storminess gathering in his employer's face he hurried on to explain the rest of it. When he was finished Barton said, 'What did you expect would happen, Frank, when you let them meet like that?'

The rangeboss fidgeted.

Bart moved over to the porch railing and eased down still looking unpleasant. He said, 'Nolan's got a horsethief up in there somewhere. That hawk-faced deputy—what's his name?'

'Jack Parton?'

'Yes. Parton. Nolan left Parton up there on the tracks and came down here to ask if we could spare a few men to help them run the horsethief down.'

Frank stared. 'Whereabouts, up there?'

'Nolan doesn't know. They've been on his trail since yesterday morning. He's a fugitive, and Nolan thinks someone is after him. He took a pair of harness-horses off a stagecoach south of town, left a worn out bay horse behind, and lit out. That's all Nolan knows.'

Barton raised his head and fixed Frank Ballinger with a skewering gaze. Frank twisted to watch the last of the riders drift into the yard, then he turned back. 'Not the line-shack,' he

133

said softly.

Barton kept staring at the *segundo*. 'Maybe not. There are miles and miles of country back in there. Dozens of trails... But if he came across the best one, the trail we use hauling supplies to the cabin...'

'Christ,' Frank said. 'I had no idea about anything like that, Bart, or I would never have let her go back up there.'

Barton softened in the face of Ballinger's agitation. 'If she'd stayed up there, or if she hadn't met Bronson and had gone back up there, she'd have been alone. Maybe this way, Frank, she's at least got help, if that horsethief finds the cabin.'

Ballinger was not concerned with possibilities. His nature required a forthright reaction to everything. He started to turn as he said, 'I'll get Ken Hill and Mike Reilly. You want that grey horse you been ridin' lately?'

Barton straightened up off the railing. 'Yes. Carbines, Frank.'

Ballinger was moving when he said, 'And lariats.'

Barton watched Frank stride hurriedly in the direction of the bunkhouse. The only possible reason Frank could have had for mentioning ropes was because he had a lynching in mind.

Barton knew about range-law. He'd seen his father return in bitter silence to the ranch several times during Barton's early years. He

134

remembered how his father had been days coming out of his shell after those affairs, but until he had been much older he had not really understood where his father had been or what had happened.

He understood how the oldtimers felt about this sort of thing. By training he agreed with the need to hang renegades, but by the rules he had learned in eastern schools he also knew this was the prerogative of the law, not the rangemen. As he watched Frank enter the bunkhouse he turned to go inside and hunt up Jenny for something to eat. He did not say a word to her, but she asked him where Beth was, and when he evaded a direct answer the black eyes fastened on his face. It irritated him; he had never been able to deceive Jenny.

'I'll be away tonight,' he told her, wolfing down food. 'I'll bring her back when I return.'

Jenny handed him a cup of black coffee. 'She wouldn't run off. Not Beth.'

Barton scowled into the coffee cup. 'She didn't leave, Jenny. Well; she's been at the line-cabin for a couple of days, and you knew that. Some of us are going up there tonight. We'll bring her back.'

The thick-bodied Indian woman with the smooth, round face of a girl, said, 'You and the men?'

'No. Frank, a couple of the riders and I. That's all.'

'And with guns?'

Barton put down the empty cup, hard. 'Jenny . . . !'

The woman stood without dropping her eyes, waiting for the angry retort which did not come. Barton looked at her, his annoyance evaporated and he smiled. 'Don't worry, Jenny.'

'Of course I'll worry. What is it—what's happened up there?'

'Sheriff Nolan was by a while ago.'

'I saw him out there with you.'

'He's hunting a horsethief in the hills. Maybe the man will go back as far as the line-cabin. That's all, Jenny. He's got hundreds of miles to sashay around in, so he may not go anywhere near the cabin. But we're going up there just in case. That's all.'

Barton wagged his head. She had always been able to pull things out of him. What irritated him now was that he hadn't been a little boy in over twenty years. He did not have to submit to this sort of thing.

Damn it, anyway.

He stepped over, roughly put an arm around her shoulders, hugged briefly, then walked back out through the house to his office where he took down a gun and shellbelt he had not worn in ages, buckled it into place, tied the thong to his leg, checked the gun for loads, then lifted down a booted Winchester from a rack of buck antlers. He got his lined jacket too, before

136

walking back to the parlour.

Jenny Plume waylaid him there with a blue cloth napkin full of food. He considered the blue cloth for a moment, then accepted the bundle—and smiled.

'Don't worry, Jenny. We'll bring her back safe and sound.'

She followed him to the veranda and waited up there in the shadows while he crossed to the barn-front where three coated men were leaning in silence beside four saddled horses. Neither Reilly nor Hill heeded Barton but at his approach they turned their animals once, snugged up the cinchas, turned them one more time then swung up. Frank waited for Barton to get astride, then he also mounted.

There were several other riders over on the bunkhouse porch, like wooden carvings. They, and Jenny Plume, watched the quartet walk their horses northeasterly out of the yard, and when they were out a ways Frank twisted in the saddle to look back. He grunted, settled forward, and put everything from his mind except what lay ahead.

Eventually he said, 'Why didn't Bob Nolan wait for us?'

Barton offered a slow, delayed reply. 'Well, probably because I wasn't very friendly toward him.' Barton felt the older man's stare and avoided meeting it. 'I told him he had no right to trespass on Senorio. I thought he had come

137

for Beth. What else was I to think?'

Frank nodded sympathetically and said no more for a considerable distance. The night was not quite fully down yet, but it would be within another couple of hours. By the time they reached the mountains and were on the line-camp trail it would be dark. There was a moon tonight, which might have helped more if they had been riding in open country, but in the forested back-country it would not help very much.

Frank was lifting his horse over into a lope when he said, 'Gawddamn mess. Did Nolan tell you he'd turned Bronson loose?'

'Yes. But by the time he'd told me that, and also that the law over at Mesquite was hot on the killer's trail, I'd already told him we would resist him with guns if we had to, to keep him from taking Beth.'

Frank said no more. They made excellent time reaching the foremost foothills. The upper Saginaw country was dead ahead, already showing nightgloom in its canyons and most thickly timbered places. This sort of thing was not something Frank approved of. Experience down the years had taught him one lesson very well—never try to force a fight with any kind of animal, two-legged or four-legged, in the dark.

But there was no choice.

Ken Hill, who had wintered at the line-cabin the last two years, knew a short-cut. Frank was

138

dubious about risking it in the night but Hill said he could do it and Frank had faith in the lanky tophand so he waved Hill on ahead.

The short-cut was steep so they had to pause often and blow the horses, but as Hill told them, it would cut about three miles off their time, and that had to be worth something.

Barton was less accustomed to saddlebacking than his companions but he did not make a sound as the horse he was riding jolted and jarred him as it followed the other horses over deadfall pines, across rocky arroyos, in and out among huge old over-ripe trees a man had to lean his head all the way to see the tops of, and finally emerged through a thorny thicket to come upon the regular trail again.

They had been an hour and a half on Ken Hill's short-cut. They had easily eliminated three miles, perhaps closer to four miles, of the regular, well-defined zig-zagging trail.

Darkness was down now, there was no moon yet, but starshine helped. It also helped that the regular trail was exposed and wide; starlight lent it an eerie, soft brightness.

It was not quite as warm at this elevation but the men had not expected the summer heat to be up here; they had all visited this area many times and they had come coated and gloved. They had also come up here with a grim resolve, and that was more nearly in their minds than a little mountain chill.

139

CHAPTER FOURTEEN

The cold which settled earlier at these higher elevations had not arrived before Walt Bronson cared for the horses in the small, emerald meadow where the line-shack was, but there were certain indications that it would eventually arrive so he carried in three armloads of wood to fill the box near the little iron stove, and Beth beamed because the wood-box had been empty and although she had been carrying in wood the last couple of days it was not a chore she enjoyed. Particularly since the men who normally lived up here never seemed to split the wood, just cut it into usable lengths and leave it like that for someone else to split.

There was plenty of food. Senorio always kept its line-cabins well provisioned. The cabin was old, it had been built during the last years of her grandfather's life. Her father had told her of coming up here with pack-mules and hired men to make the cabin, which in those days had also doubled as a hunting lodge; back in those days cattle were too valuable to eat, they were raised to sell so the ranchers would have some hard money; people lived off wild meat. But Senorio's riders had only used the cabin since Beth could remember, to ride out from in the late autumn and winter and keep cattle or horses from drifting out of the country.

Walt was impressed by the stout fir walls, the mighty, draw-knifed rafters, and the painstakingly created two-foot-long sugarpine snakes on the roof. He laughed when he told her he would settle for something this good when he finally decided to settle down—and missed the odd look she gave him.

When the sun had departed a pigeon-toed old boar bear went shambling across the meadow below the cabin, and without once looking around at the consternation he had caused, left the horses in quaking panic as his furry rear-end disappeared through the trees, beyond which several miles distant, he had his special preserve. He clearly had only one thought in mind—to get to his bed-ground before it got dark.

Walt stood outside smoking, keeping an eye on the horses until they settled down again, then listened to the bumbling progress of the old bear until he was no longer audible. When he turned, Beth was in the doorway. He smiled. 'You'd sure make a downright handsome pioneer's wife,' he said, and moved closer.

'If you were the pioneer,' she said, then, perhaps chagrined at her boldness, turned swiftly back inside where she had been preparing supper at the little wood-stove. When he closed the door and went over to watch, she blew upward from the corner of her mouth to force an unruly heavy coil of hair upwards, and smiled at him. 'When was the last time you ate?'

He did not give her a direct answer, he instead wrinkled his nose in exaggerated ecstasy. 'Never, when it smelled this good nor had been cooked by such a beautiful *cosinero*.' For a long moment they looked steadily at one another; the cabin was snug, warm, and private. It was secluded and there was a long night ahead. Their thoughts were very similar without either of them knowing it. Then a horse whinnied.

The unsettling moment was destroyed. Walt went to the door because there were no windows, and looked out. Both her black and his bay were standing with their heads up and their ears pointing. Walt could see nothing beyond the meadow, and soon now he would be unable to see even that far. There was nothing visible which had not been there earlier, but it bothered him that the horses were still motionless, peering toward the far fringe of trees. They would not have whinnied at anything except another horse, or possibly a mule, but they would not have made a sound if they had scented wild game or cattle.

Nor were they afraid, so whatever was holding them motionless was not a wild predator. Walt reached inside the door for the Winchester leaning there, and Beth saw him do that. She came to the doorway to lean and look

142

past.

Walt quietly said, 'Stay inside. Bar the door after me.'

She raised a set of fingers to his arm. 'What is it?'

'I don't know. Maybe someone's stray horse, but this is a long way from grass for a horse to drift.'

She still clung to him. 'A rider?'

He simply shook his head to indicate that he had not the faintest idea. Beth released her hold. 'Frank, possibly. He knew we'd be up here.'

Walt remained silent. If that had been Frank Ballinger he would have ridden on in. Whoever was out there either had seen the cabin, had perhaps detected the aroma of cooking a mile off and was still riding toward the clearing, or it was someone who was being deliberately careful before they showed themselves, and that possibility was foremost in Walt's mind when he gently eased her back and repeated what he had just said. 'Bar the door after me and stay inside.' Then, at the look on her face, he also said, 'It's probably nothing. I'll be back in a few minutes.'

She watched him go around the cabin on her left, closed the door only after he had disappeared around there, and the moon sailed from among some tattered clouds to cast a ghostly glow over the house, the meadow, and the distant dark timber.

Nothing moved out there. The horses were

still fascinated by something they could scent but which they could not see. Walt took his bearings from the direction they were watching, but he went from the rear of the house into the timber first, then began skirting on around, being as silent as he could be.

Moonlight penetrated the timber at intervals where line-shack-riders had cut wood down the years. Walt avoided those open places, kept to their outskirts, and took all the time he thought he might need to get southward.

Once, he heard a stamping sound, and confident it would be a horse, was nearly run over by an antlered buck deer who had been startled out of his bed.

After that he paused, leaned against a red fir tree and waited. If there were other deer in the area he wanted them to either hear or smell him, and clear out. While he was standing there a soft sound of unmistakable footfalls came like a whisper from over on his right. The hair at the back of Walt's neck stood up. That was not Frank Ballinger; Frank would not be moving as stealthily as this man was. Frank would have no reason to.

Walt twisted from the waist to trace out the exact location of that stalker. He did not see the man, but he could guess what the stranger was doing—he had seen the cabin and was now very stealthily circling around to get up behind it. Indignation more than any other emotion motivated Walt to step forth very gently and soundlessly, to start stalking the stranger. If that was someone else besides Frank from Senorio, he was going to get a surprise. Only after Walt had been moving with infinite care not to make a sound, did it occur to him that no one from Senorio knew he was up here. They might know Beth was, and they might know she was alone up here, miles from help of any kind.

It did not occur to him that the faint, grey silhouette he was eventually able to make out, was as much a stranger to the Saginaw back-country as Walt also was. When he could see the man halt in the trees behind the cabin, and straighten up a little as he peered down at the line-shack, it finally crossed his mind that this was a complete stranger. He was a man about Walt's size and build, but with hair which hung almost to his shoulders, and a dark-shading of beard stubble. He had a Colt on his right hip, and in the weak moonlight the grips dully shone. It was an ivory-handled sixgun, but the man had a carbine in his hands as he stood, leaning slightly, as he peered ahead.

Walt's concern was to protect Beth. There was a spiral of smoke rising from the cabin stove-pipe so the stranger knew someone was down there. The man looked wild, unkempt and furtive. He probably had not seen a pretty woman in a long while, and finding one up here, ostensibly alone, would probably appear as an unexpected bonus to him.

Walt's ultimate assessment was that the stalker was a renegade. He looked it and he acted it. Then the man turned slightly and studied the pair of horses, Walt's bay and Beth's black.

Walt waited a moment longer, until the stranger shifted his position a little in order to make a better appraisal of the hobbled horses, then Walt eased soundlessly in beside a big tree and started to raise the carbine. Whether the stranger meant to sneak down to the cabin, or turn aside now that he had satisfied himself the cabin was occupied, and attempt to steal their horses, he was hostile, and that mattered above anything else, even a possible logical explanation about the stranger's presence up here.

Walt leaned to take a rest with his left hand so that he could place the carbine across his knuckles, and the stranger suddenly moved. He was in plain sight one moment, the next moment he had a large tree on his right side, between himself and Bronson. Walt took his gun-rest and waited.

The renegade came back into sight, very briefly, as he began working his way northward deeper in among the trees, and Walt had to shift his stance, had to sidle around his tree to prevent the other man from looking down there and seeing him.

146

Apparently the renegade was not going down to the cabin after all. He kept circling around, moving faster now, and making small noises as he swung in and out among the trees on his way up and around, and back down to the area where the trees grew closest to where the horses were grazing.

Walt had to re-trace his steps. He guessed that the renegade had only scouted up the cabin to satisfy himself that whoever was inside was unlikely to come out, or that no one was already outside. Now, the renegade's real purpose became clear. He was going to steal a horse— perhaps two horses.

Walt had an advantage. The renegade was farther back in the trees. Walt only had to remain down closer to the little meadow to cover the same ground as the pair of them moved back to the west side of the meadow.

But Walt also had to be more careful now than he had been before because the stranger was able to watch the easterly timber, down where Walt was. The pale night-gloom was on Walt's side. He eventually got into position about where he guessed the renegade would come down to the edge of the clearing, crept into a thicket, and waited.

He did not see the man but he heard him coming. In fact he did not see the man even when he passed within a hundred feet of Walt's thicket. Then the renegade halted, Walt eased aside some leafy limbs, caught the pale reflection of that ivory pistol-grip, and because the man was now standing in layers of darkness Walt had to minutely make out the leaning silhouette where the renegade had grounded his saddle-gun and was leaning on it.

The renegade was relaxed for the first time since Walt had seen him. He was looking out at the horses as though in the process of deciding which one he meant to take.

It was Walt Bronson's best chance thus far in all their manoeuvering. He leaned aside his carbine very gently, reached slowly for his holstered Colt, had the gun clearing leather when from a distance, muted by the trees and space, a faint sound as of horses moving was instantly detected by the renegade. The man jerked straight up, suddenly intensely alert and wary again. He looked southward where that sound had come from.

Walt painstakingly lifted his gun-arm. He said, 'Don't move!'

The stranger was like a coiled spring. He sprang aside and twisted toward the sound of Walt's voice as he was in the air. The man dropped his saddlegun and as Walt squeezed off a shot the man moved. The bullet made a solid, meaty sound where it struck a pine bole about three feet from the stranger. The man did not stop moving. He drew and fired with incredible speed, but he had no target, only a general area.

even so the bullet cut underbrush within a yard of Walt, and the advantage now swung to the renegade. Walt was not visible but his gun-flash had been, and he was in the middle of a thicket where he could move very little.

He tracked the moving renegade as the man turned to swiftly retreat back among the trees, and fired. The stranger swung and fired back. Walt could see movement and little else as the distance between them widened. He raised his gun, sighted a foot ahead of where the renegade was withdrawing, leading the renegade the way hunters lead fleeing game, and fired.

The renegade faltered, then fell. Walt's mouth was as dry as cotton. He waited a long time for the renegade to move, to fire back, to do anything at all.

Those distant moving horses were no longer audible but from the west a new sound came. It could have been a disturbed wild animal, but if it was, it was a large one because the sound was of something large pushing through underbrush. And it was moving toward Walt, not away from him which would have been the case had it been a wild animal.

Walt decided that man lying up ahead was not going to fire, and began to punch out spent casings from his Colt and push in fresh loads from his shellbelt. When he had finished, the renegade still had not moved.

Walt stood up in a crouch, stepped out of his

149

thicket, pressed behind a tree, waited a few moments, then stepped boldly around where he could see the prone man. There still was no movement. He went forward, always with a convenient large tree on one side or the other, and came up close enough to be able to make out the stranger.

The man was lying on his side as though at rest. His hat was a few feet away and his ivory-stocked sixgun was lying under a relaxed hand. Walt cocked his gun, stepped over and leaned. The man was dead. His features were completely relaxed, all the furtiveness was gone. Walt had no idea where the bullet had struck, it was too dark among the trees to be sure about that, but there was no doubt about one thing; he had killed the renegade.

CHAPTER FIFTEEN

One of the hobbled horses nickered and Walt whirled away from the renegade to fade into tree-darkness. Now, that sound from the west which had been parallel to where the renegade was lying, was no longer audible, but as Walt remained utterly still he caught a blur of fluid movement. It was a man, and within moments another blurry silhouette appeared. One of them was north of Walt, the other one was south of him. They were picking their ways forward toward the meadow with Walt between them.

These two were as furtive as the renegade had been. Walt re-gripped his sixgun and scarcely breathed. Neither of the oncoming men seemed to suspect Walt was close by, but evidently the recent furious exchange of gunshots had made them extremely wary.

Walt guessed they were friends of the renegade. He had no reason to believe otherwise, and when the man south of him finally stepped up parallel with Walt, but several yards southward with a diffused glow of starlight around him where there was a break in trees, the man suddenly turned as though he had heard something to the south, and Walt could not see his face despite the starlight.

He swung to look for the other one, but evidently that man had also decided to halt; he was nowhere in sight.

Walt turned back to the first one he had seen. The man was still looking southward. Walt tested the pine-needles, found them as spongily soft underfoot as he had expected, and took four big strides to get closer to the visible stranger.

Finally, he too heard horses to the south of the clearing, down where the trail made its final curve before entering the meadow. The sounds were stronger now, as though whoever was down there, after having been driven to a halt at the outbreak of sudden gunfire, was now coming on again.

The stranger did not turn to flee as the dead man had done. He remained motionless and watching. Walt took another four long steps, got close enough, and held his breath as he took one more step which brought him up behind, and slightly to one side, of the stranger before he swung his gunbarrel in an overhand arc. The stranger's hat was driven down over his ears as the man dropped without even a gasp.

Walt sank to one knee looking over his shoulder for the other one, saw no sign of him and turned back to flop the unconscious stranger onto his back and yank off his hat.

It was Sheriff Bob Nolan!

Walt recoiled. To his left, horsemen began infiltrating the trees. Walt heard the abrasive sound of rubbing leather. He turned slowly, still shocked about the identity of the man he had cold-cocked, and saw a lean, rawboned silhouette which sat loosely erect in his saddle. A second horseman was filtering through farther to the west. As this man passed across a ghostly clearing Walt recognised him. The rider was gazing off on his right down toward the clearing. It was Ken Hill.

Walt stood up beside Sheriff Nolan, moved over beside a bull-pine and when that lanky, easy-riding man came along Walt raised his Colt and stepped directly into the horseman's path.

It was Frank Ballinger. He halted and sat

staring from Walt's face to the upraised, cocked Colt. Then he turned aside, spat, turned back and said, 'What was all the shootin' about?' as quietly and casually as though they had been together this night, up in here.

Walt lowered the gun, eased off the hammer and used the gun as a pointer. 'I don't know who he was, but he's lying over yonder. He was skulkin' around. I think he was after the horses.'

Frank swung to earth and nearly stumbled over Bob Nolan. He recoiled with a gasp, then looked up. 'You shot the sheriff, for Chris'sake, Bronson!'

'No. The dead one's over yonder. I just hit the sheriff over the head. I thought he was another renegade.'

Frank dropped his reins and moved carefully ahead until he found the dead man. He lifted his voice and called to the other riders, then he knelt to examine the dead man. As Walt walked up the rangeboss said, 'Where's Beth?'

Walt jerked his head in the direction of the cabin. 'Inside with the door barred.'

That stalking man Walt had seen northward through the trees came soundlessly down and halted where he caught his first glance of the dead man. He was a pale-haired, burly man with a deputy sheriff's badge on his jacket. He looked up at Walt, half scowling. 'Bronson?'

Walt nodded.

'I'm Jack Parton, deputy from Marietta. Sheriff Nolan and I been hunting a horsethief.' Parton moved over where Frank was stiffly arising from his kneeling position beside the dead man. Parton looked, leaned for a closer look and said, 'Hell, this is him,' to Frank, but the rangeboss turned without a word and pointed. 'Nolan's lying yonder,' he said.

The deputy swiftly crossed in front of Walt, and two other men came along, Ken Hill and Mike Reilly. The last man to come up, still on his horse, was Barton Archer. He ignored Walt to look at the dead man. Frank was already moving away, out in the direction of the meadow and on across it to the line-cabin.

Walt would have gone with him but that hawk-faced deputy was coming back toward him looking furious. 'Who hit the sheriff?' he demanded.

Walt replied evenly. 'I did. I'd nailed this feller and saw two more of 'em coming. One down there, the other one up yonder in the direction you came from. I figured they were this man's partners.'

Barton Archer joined Hill and Reilly gazing at the corpse. Deputy Parton stood glowering, then, without another word he turned back to care for the groaning sheriff. Evidently Bob Nolan had a thick skull, because Walt had hit him hard enough to keep most men unconscious for another fifteen or twenty minutes.

Barton walked over to Walt. 'Is Beth all right?'

Walt nodded. 'She's inside with the door barred.' They both turned to head for the cabin. Behind them Ken Hill said, 'Hey Jack—is this the feller you were lookin' for?'

Deputy Parton sounded disagreeable when he replied. 'Yeah, that's the son of a bitch. Nolan's got a wanted dodger in his pocket with that feller's picture on it.'

Hill said, 'He's the one robbed two horses off Martin Steven's stagecoach?'

'Yeah. The sheriff and I found those two horses about a mile southeast of here, rode down . . . And that's not all he's wanted for. They've had a posse lookin' high and low for him down south.'

Hill said, 'Well, this sure isn't south, Jack.'

'No. I figure the son of a bitch saw all the manhunters down there lookin' for him, and cut back up in this direction.'

Mike Reilly, who had been following this exchange, had a question for the deputy sheriff. 'What did he do that they was after him for?'

'Robbed the bank over at Mesquite, and killed a cashier durin' the robbery,' stated Parton. Then he also said, 'Any of you fellers got some whiskey for the sheriff?'

Walt stopped in his tracks and looked back where the conversing men were. At his side,

Barton Archer said, 'Nolan didn't tell me that down at the ranch,' and walked on over to the cabin where Frank and Beth were standing.

Hill and Reilly went methodically to care for the horses, moving with the phlegmatic attitude of men who did something like this from habit and without thinking about it. Deputy Parton finally got Sheriff Nolan on his feet and was helping him toward the cabin.

Walt saw Beth's searching glance as he moved into the orange light of the cabin doorway, and smiled. She left Frank and Barton to walk out to him, and without any self-consciousness at all, she raised her arms to his shoulders, pressed close and buried her face against his chest as she said, 'Thank God,' and clung to him.

Frank stood like a rawboned statue looking on. It was not possible in that poor light with his back to the cabin door to make out the feelings reflected in his craggy face, but Barton Archer at his side, said, 'Jenny'll be pleased,' and Frank turned slowly to gaze at his employer. 'About what; Beth bein' all right?'

'That too, but she's been privately telling me for several years now that Beth needed a husband and a family more than she needed me—or Senorio.'

Frank stepped aside as Jack Parton guided Sheriff Nolan into the warm and lighted cabin. As they passed along and the sheriff looked upwards from watery eyes, Frank unsympathetically said, 'Serves you right,' and turned with a sign to go out where Hill and Reilly were caring for the livestock.

Photoset, printed and bound in Great Britain by
REDWOOD BURN LIMITED, Trowbridge, Wiltshire
157

ACB
C-17->W